CHARLIE'S WILL

SUSAN MACKIE

STP
SMALL TOWN PUBLISHING

For my girls
Jas, Emi and little Olive

Do you drive by old homes and wonder about the lives of those that built them, lived there, loved and lost?

Writers tell such stories. Sometimes real, sometimes imagined. Often both.

— SUSAN MACKIE

1

A fine layer of red-brown dust settled on the windscreen as Rose followed the line of slow-moving vehicles from the cemetery to the homestead. So much dust – more than she'd ever seen here. It hadn't rained in months. She braked as the line slowed. Her Jeep was the last vehicle in an odd line-up that was a perfect summary of Charlie's wide circle of friends. Battered farm vehicles, an ancient Fairlane with a throaty eight-cylinder purr and freshly-washed late-model cars belonging to town folk trailed each other sluggishly up the driveway.

Rose left her dusty red Jeep down by the stables and walked to the homestead, needing a few minutes to gather her composure. As Charlie's only living relative she felt an overwhelming sense of responsibility, and duty, wash over her. She was truly alone now the last of her blood was in the ground, and faced difficult decisions in the coming days and weeks.

'Barrington' was a grand old home, built in 1895 by Rose's great-great-grandfather, Scottish immigrant Alexander Gordon, for his wife, the first Rose Gordon. An ancient golden ash stood sentinel a short distance from the front door, its leaves beginning to turn in the early March sunshine.

The stately home presided over an oasis of green lawn and native shrubs, wattle and bottle-brush in bloom, with tea roses flowering down each side of the path leading to the wide stone steps. The late afternoon air was thick with the scent of roses and buzzing bees, darting from blossoms to lavender bushes planted to one side. The wide veranda stretched around the building and heavy rosewood double doors stood open to the polished hardwood floor of the spacious entrance hall.

Sitting in the front pew of the church alone, Rose had barely nodded to the concerned faces around her, some familiar and many not. Now she hesitated on the threshold; listening to the rise and fall of dozens of voices, settling in for the wake. Snippets of conversation drifted by as she entered the sitting room, open to the formal lounge and dining areas for the occasion.

"Charlie had a good innings. Eighty-three and still riding that cranky old stallion of his. I thought he'd kill himself on that horse, not go from a stroke ..."

"... he was a cheeky blighter, always had a yarn to tell ..."

"...the first one to bring a truckload of hay when the shed burnt down ... would never have survived that winter without it ..."

Charlie Gordon had been well liked, and respected in the district and beyond. He had been quick to help a neighbour in need, provide cattle for the camp draft and hay bales for seating at local events. He had been a cattle and horse judge at district shows and had done a couple of terms on local Council. His forthright manner and strong family values had made him an unofficial arbitrator when friends or neighbours had disagreements. Charlie Gordon had been able to get to the heart of a problem in few words and had a way of helping others find their own solutions. Rose was proud to be his grand-daughter.

It was true she'd rarely been home to visit in the last couple of years. Busy with her own life and work in Sydney, she phoned every week, but that was not a replacement for a visit, she admonished herself. When she'd come home briefly at Christmas he'd seemed quieter, more introspective. He'd missed his beloved Vera deeply after her grandmother had passed the year before. However, he'd held himself ramrod straight and managed the farm with a little help and attended personally to the house yard and gardens, rampant with his departed wife's champion roses.

Walking through the room, Rose acknowledged murmurs of condolence and questions about how long would she stay and she must drop by for lunch and a chat. The CWA ladies were busy in the kitchen, serving platters of homemade scones, cakes and biscuits. Plenty of tea and coffee was on offer, yet Rose noticed some older men had opened a bottle of port and were toasting her grandfather.

"To Charlie."

"To Charlie. May his girth-strap stay firm and his saddle never shift".

"To Charlie".

Mrs Tait from the farm next door set down the tray of scones and sandwiches she held and swept Rose into a tight hug against her ample chest. "Oh Rosie love, so sad to have Charlie pass like that and so soon after your dear grandmother. You will have a lot to deal with over the next days and weeks, but know that we are close by. Call on us for anything you need."

Squeezing her back in acknowledgement, Rose smiled sadly. "Thank you. It's comforting to know how well respected Charlie was in the community."

"Not just Charlie, love. Even though you've been away a few years, you are as much a part of Barrington as Charlie. Anything we would do for him, we offer to you." Mrs Tait patted Rose gently on the shoulder. "I've put casseroles in the fridge to get you by for the next couple of days, plus fresh eggs, bread and milk. You'll have leftover sandwiches and slice after today, too." Mrs Tait nodded toward the tray she had set down.

The kind words were almost her undoing and Rose swallowed a sob, turning it into a hiccup to hide the rawness she felt. Now wasn't the time. Later – later she could grieve. Turning back into the room, she cleared her throat loudly. Within moments the chatter had quietened, and all looked expectantly at Rose.

"Thank you all for coming today, for honouring Charlie in this way. He wasn't much of a speech-maker himself, so I will simply say that his funeral service and wake has been exactly as he would have liked. Please raise your glasses." Rose accepted a glass of port from old Mr Saunders and raised it.

"To Charlie."

All in the room raised the glass or cup in their hand toward Rose while Mr Saunders, a baritone, broke into a stirring rendition of *Auld Lang Syne*, the entire room joining in after the first line *"should auld acquaintance be forgot ..."*

THE AFTERNOON WAS WANING as friends and neighbours began to take their leave. Rose slipped out to the back veranda, determined to keep her tears at bay. Despite the large attendance at the funeral, she had never felt so alone. Charlie had been her only living relative and her loss was palpable. Fiercely ambitious, Rose had left home to attend university at eighteen. She knew she often hesitated to get close to people, preferring to keep most as acquaintances and few as friends. Living in Sydney all these years she had never experienced the sense of community she had grown up with, yet knew her focus on career and independence had pushed some, who may have become closer, away. Somehow, she always thought Charlie would be here for her. His death had been a shock.

Dusk created shadows in the garden and she could hear cars driving unhurriedly back down the poplar-lined driveway to the main road to town. She called to Ruff, her grandfather's old border collie, laying on the veranda. He got to his feet and ambled over, leaning against her leg for a pat. "You're getting on too, old boy," she whispered.

Kneeling down, she buried her face in the old dog's fur and sobbed. She pictured Ruff always at Charlie's side, trotting at his heel as he walked to the yards, laying by his feet while he gardened and out here on the veranda, his head often resting on Charlie's knee while he smoked his pipe. Rose would never see Charlie again, hear his voice, listen to his stories and feel his warm gaze, always so proud of her, on her face.

A movement to one side, where the veranda was already in deep shadow, caught her eye. Rose flinched as a tall male unfolded himself from Charlie's favourite wicker patio chair.

"Who are you? What are you doing out here? The wake is inside." She stood ramrod straight, wiped her eyes with the back of one hand, irritated to discover a stranger making himself comfortable in her grandfather's domain and embarrassed to be caught crying.

"Angus Hamilton. And you are Rose. Pleased to meet you, Charlie talked about you a lot." He held out his hand to shake hers. "I am very sorry for your loss." Rose strode over, took his hand and shook it firmly, looking up at his tanned face, blue eyes and thick dark hair. She had noticed him at the funeral, briefly wondered who he was. Rose quickly took in long, lean legs in tight moleskins and quality chambray shirt; long sleeves undone and rolled to the elbow. Broad shoulders, she registered, then pulled her hand from his.

"Did he? Well I have to say, he didn't mention you at all. How did you know Charlie?" she demanded, unaware she had drawn herself up to her full height, five foot eight, stuck her chin out a little and pulled her shoulders back, her eyes challenging his for an answer. She winced when old Ruff trotted over to the man and leaned against his knee, seeking affection. He was obviously a frequent visitor for Ruff to know him so well. Turning her grief to anger was better than breaking down in front of this stranger.

When he didn't immediately respond, instead looking at her intently, his gaze lingering on her long legs, moving up to her eyes, now darkened with anger. Rose snapped, "If you are done looking me over like a heifer at the market, Mr Hamilton, can you please explain your connection?" Rose was furious. She knew he was checking her out, assessing her. What right did he have? She was accustomed to looks from men. Sometimes she found it amusing. Not today.

"I have this day buried my grandfather. You are in his house, sitting in his chair as if you have a right to and you dare look me over! Please leave. Don't bother with an explanation, I am no longer interested," Rose walked to the door and held it open, molten anger dripping with every word, every gesture.

Angus looked down as he slowly gave old Ruff a scratch across his shoulders. Charlie was right. He'd said Rose is a cracker of a girl. He had taken in her aggressive posture; the angry tilt of her head, her strong features and wavy, dark auburn hair falling across her shoulders. Strong handshake too. Definitely Charlie's granddaughter. Her deep brown eyes looked almost black. Charlie said she had a temper. He wanted to smile at that but hesitated to anger her further, fully aware he had interrupted a private moment of grief. Instead, he picked up his Akubra hat from the floor by the chair and walked past her, doffing it as he left.

He needed to talk to her, owed Charlie that much at least, but it was obvious now was not the time. Somewhat disappointed that their meeting had not gone well, he walked through the house, nodding to some as he left, shaking a hand here and there, before striding outside to his vehicle. He sat for a moment, looking at the beautiful old homestead and her lovely gardens, as the sun began to sink behind her.

Shaking his head, he started up and drove slowly out. A conversation with Rose Gordon will need to be had, whether she likes it or not.

Finally alone, Rose went back to the veranda and curled up in the wicker chair with a glass of port in one hand, the other resting on Ruff's head. She let the tears flow. What would she do without Charlie? He was the last of her family. Her grandmother was gone and her parents had died six years ago, within six months of each other.

Her mother's aggressive breast cancer had taken them all by surprise when Rose was finishing her first year of Uni. She came home to help nurse her through a double mastectomy and chemotherapy, but it was too little too late as the doctors had warned. They stopped treatment in the last two months and tried to make her as comfortable as they could. Rose read aloud and watched many movies, mostly romantic comedies and old fashioned musicals, laying beside her mother on her bed. The time they had was precious. Rose smiled sadly recalling how her mother's thin face lit up when her father came into the sickroom to spend time with her. It had always been like that, the two of them so close, almost to the exclusion of all else.

While they became accustomed to the concept of her mother's death, she planned her own funeral right down to the hymns to be sung and the roses on her casket, the loss of her father just six months later was a shock to Rose and her grandparents. Jim Gordon had been sad, but coping, although he often disappeared for days at a time. The death certificate declared he died in a car accident, but Rose secretly believed he had taken his own life, not wanting to settle for a life without his beloved Helen.

Thinking about it fuelled a primal anger within her. Had he loved her at all? She could understand his grief, but his act had left Rose an orphan. Her grandparents had always been there, but it was not the same. The farm seemed empty without her parents. It was nothing without her grandparents.

Rose had a meeting scheduled tomorrow with Douglas Barlow, Charlie's Solicitor, to sort out the will. He had spoken to her briefly at the cemetery and asked her to call him. She would have to sell the homestead and farm; she could think of no other option. Even without her publishing career, apartment and life in Sydney, she couldn't run the farm by herself. Two thousand acres of prime farmland, around 400 head of beef cattle, grain and hay crops and the horses her grandfather loved so much.

He had sold some of the stock before his death and most of the horses; keeping only his old stallion, Topper, two mares in foal and a filly he was beginning to break in. Perhaps the Tait family from next door have an interest in the property? She recalled her grandfather mentioning that young Jamie Tait was getting married. Would they be in a position to acquire more land? The drought was taking its toll and not many would have ready cash; she knew.

She sighed sadly. No point speculating. She would speak to Barlow tomorrow and make a plan from there.

AT TEN MINUTES to nine Rose strode through the doors of what used to be the Bank of New South Wales, a substantial brick edifice built in the mid-nineteenth century, housing the law offices of Barlow and Maxwell upstairs and a recently opened funky alfresco style coffee shop downstairs.

Rose barely glanced at the coffee shop as she went by, her head high and back straight. She didn't see the young woman behind the counter start toward her with a tea towel in one hand and a slight smile on her face. The woman hesitated and Rose was on her way up the polished timber staircase before she had taken a second step. The young woman smiled at a customer as she glanced back to where Rose had been, just moments before.

Rose hadn't been in this building since her father's death, so soon after her mother. She was nineteen at the time, but she remembered having her beloved grandparents on each side of her as they climbed these stairs to hear her father's will. She hadn't cried publicly then either, preferring to contain her grief until she was alone.

Taking the stairs two at a time, her riding boots made a satisfying clopping noise on the worn treads of the rosewood steps. Rose hoped Mr Barlow did not mind her arriving in jeans and a pale blue cotton shirt, looking somewhat casual for what was, of course, a solemn discussion. She had been down to the stables before breakfast and fed and groomed Topper, her grandfather's irascible old stallion, and after showering had changed into riding gear intending to tour the farm after the meeting in town. The stallion had been her grandfather's pride and joy, but looked out of condition and she wondered when he had last been ridden. Not for weeks, if she was any judge.

Stopping short when she entered the solicitor's rooms, Rose smiled at Mrs Barlow behind the front desk. Frances Barlow had been her husband's receptionist and secretary for over 35 years and locals believed she was as knowledgeable about law as her husband and his partner, Thomas Maxwell. Frances looked up from her computer and seeing Rose, stood and walked briskly around the desk, a warm smile of welcome on her lips. A small, well-dressed woman, she gave off a comforting aura of trustworthiness and a hint of Chanel Number Five.

"Rose, so nice to see you. I wanted to speak to you at the church yesterday, but it seemed you had enough to deal with there. This is never easy, but please understand that Douglas and I are here for you, in and out of this office, at any time for any reason. Would you like to come to dinner at our home tomorrow night?" As she spoke, Frances touched Rose's arm lightly, emphasising the sincerity of her words.

"Thank you Mrs Barlow, I would like that. You acted for three generations of our family, and I know you were in my grandfather's confidence. I may need advice in coming weeks, on how to progress," Rose smiled down at the older woman.

"Right. That's settled, Come at six pm tomorrow night. And Rose...?"

"Yes."

"Please call us by our first names."

Rose smiled again. "Thank you, Frances."

Frances walked to the large cedar door of her husband's office, opened it, and gestured for Rose to enter.

"I'll bring in a pot of tea, Douglas," Frances nodded to her husband behind his ancient timber desk. It had very little on it; just one manila file, a notepad, the phone and a computer to one side. There was another desk against the wall that was covered with files tied together by red ribbons, in neat piles, as Rose remembered. There would not be a scrap of dust; Frances would not allow that.

Rose smiled warmly at her grandfather's lawyer, his thick head of hair now quite grey but his hazel eyes bright and interested. He stood as Rose walked further into the room.

Frances closed the door as she left.

Walking toward Douglas behind his large old desk, Rose stopped, startled, when she saw another person sitting to one side. The angle of the open door had hidden him. She exhaled in horror.

"You!"

Rose was confused for a moment. Why would Angus Hamilton, the stranger from last night, be here, now? She turned to Douglas Barlow, mentally pulling herself together.

"Sorry, I must have the wrong time since you are busy. I'm not sure why Frances showed me in." She nodded to Douglas and without another glance at Angus, strode toward the door.

"Rose, wait." Douglas spoke in his usual quiet, considered manner. "Angus is here for the reading of your grandfather's will. I am sorry, I thought Charlie had discussed this with you some time ago. I know he intended to talk to you about it."

Working hard not to show how shocked she was, Rose

turned around. "My grandfather may have been waiting to speak to me in person. I've not been home since Christmas."

Stepping over to the remaining chair in front of the lawyer's desk, Rose sat, crossing her long, denim-clad legs. With great self-control she nodded to the lawyer and said "Please continue Mr Barlow."

During this exchange, Angus Hamilton had risen from his chair.

"Please stay Miss Gordon. I will leave. You should have this conversation in private. I had no idea you were unaware of your grandfather's plans." He nodded to Rose, then the lawyer, and was at the door in two large steps.

"Angus. Thank you, I will speak to you later," Barlow said quietly as Frances re-entered the room bearing a tray with a teapot, milk jug and three fine china cups. She tried to hide her surprise as Angus held the door open for her, before leaving the room.

Rose kept her breathing steady as she looked directly at Douglas Barlow. She could feel tears gathering and did not want to shed them. Not here. Not now.

"Please read my grandfather's will, Mr Barlow, I have taken up enough of your time today."

Douglas Barlow looked at her kindly, drew several type-written pages from the file on his desk and began reading aloud.

4

Angus walked slowly down the stairs to the street, where he hesitated before entering the café.

"Hi Angus, your usual?" the young woman from the café asked.

"Yes, thanks Deb."

Angus perched on a stool at the counter while he waited for his coffee. He shook his head, trying to dislodge the feeling that he was somehow in the wrong. Why would Charlie not have told his grand-daughter about his will? Charlie knew his heart was failing, had wanted to lock in the details. He had certainly made Angus very aware of his intentions.

Did this change anything? Legally? Morally? He wished he knew the best way to progress. The right way. Douglas Barlow would, no doubt, call him back in later in the day. Until then, he had better get to work.

"Here you go. One double shot extra-large long black, with

a dash of cream." He took his coffee and smiled at the young woman as he stood up.

"Think this weather will break anytime soon?" she nodded to the clear blue sky, the day already uncomfortably warm.

"Wish it would, Deb. We badly need rain. So many are doing it tough. I heard they are trucking hay up from down near Adelaide to feed stock here. The cost of freight alone makes it hardly worth it. Old Saunders is shutting his dairy at the end of the month, selling off the stock in milk and the breeders. Sad. Fifth generation dairy-farmer. He is hoping that will give him enough breathing space to hang on to the young ones for beef production. Only a few big dairies left in the district now, Saunders was the last of the small ones."

"Do you think he will sell out to the consortium, now he has stopped milking? His boy was never interested and the grand-kids rarely visit."

Angus paused for a moment before he answered. "I don't know. Saunders was close to old Charlie and he was dead against the consortium buying up prime farming land in the area. I reckon Saunders will hang on if he can."

Angus shook his head as Deb went to serve another customer. If multi-generational farmers like Saunders can't make a go of it, what hope does a young farmer have?

5

J ust over an hour later Rose walked heavily down the stairs, shocked and bewildered. With stomach churning, she stepped out next to the café bustling with mid-morning customers. She did not register the aroma of coffee or the laughter of a group of young mothers in one corner, happily chatting to each other with babies on their laps.

Walking toward her car parked outside the cafe, Rose finally turned when her name was called for the third time.

The young woman from the coffee shop stood before her, tucking a lock of thick blond hair behind her ear. There was a worried smile on her pretty face, flushed from the steam of the coffee maker. Rose hesitated for a moment, registering the person before her.

"Debbie?! Debbie Webb!" Rose threw her arms around her old friend. They each spoke at once.

"Rose. I was so sorry to hear about your grandfather. I sent flowers and a card and came to the church, although it was such a big funeral I am not surprised you did not see me there. I planned to come out to the farm after work today," Debbie gestured back toward the coffee shop counter.

"Debbie! I had no idea you were back from London; I would have looked out for you. My last email bounced, and I was going to speak to your Mum next time I came home to catch up on your news."

Rose lowered her voice, "I haven't read through the cards yet. I know I should .... I'm sorry."

"It's OK Rose. I've been back for months. I'm engaged." Debbie thrust her left hand out for Rose to see the white gold ring with six twinkling low set diamonds.

"Wow! Engaged! Congratulations!" Rose felt genuine happiness for her friend. They had been inseparable during high school and their first year at university. Rose had studied Communications, Debbie Physiotherapy, and they had planned to go to London together. When Rose's mother was diagnosed with breast cancer, Rose insisted Debbie go to London, anyway. Then her mother died, and her father not long after. It was a terrible time. She'd thrown herself into completing her studies, intending to go to London after that. Then an opportunity came up in a Sydney publishing house. Rose took it. After that they seemed to email and Skype less and Rose knew in her heart that it was she who had let the friendship slide. Deep down, she was envious that Debbie had followed through with their shared dream.

"You haven't asked who I am engaged to ..." Debbie said.

Rose stood back from her friend, looking into her happy face. Always such a pretty girl, but radiant today.

"Tell me," Rose demanded.

"Jamie Tait." Debbie giggled.

"Jamie!" Rose laughed. "The boy next door. We used to beg him to let us play cowboys and Indians with him and his brother. The beasts, remember how they always made us Indians and would tie us to a tree and run off and leave us? For hours!" They were both laughing now.

"Remember when Charlie wanted to untie us, but we insisted we were part of the game and the 'cowboys' would be back! Then he told us the boys were at the house, drinking hot chocolate and eating your grandmother's sponge cake."

"But we got them back. Many times..." They were both laughing so much that the group of young mothers had stopped chatting and were watching, smiling.

Rose straightened up and wiped the tears of laughter from her eyes. Debbie! How wonderful. It felt so good to laugh with an old friend and remember less complicated times. And she was marrying a local and staying in town.

"I have to get back to work, but here's my mobile number." Debbie thrust a piece of notepaper torn from an order book into Rose's hand. "We haven't had a proper engagement party; we are planning something small next Saturday out at Jamie's parents' farm. You have to come."

"I'd love to. I don't have to go back to Sydney for another week, so it's perfect." Rose smiled.

"Oh. You're not staying? I thought you might stay...?"

"I only have two weeks off work, but turns out it's more complicated than I expected." Rose shrugged, and Debbie wisely chose not to ask further questions in that moment. She knew from old that Rose was struggling to keep her emotions in check and would not like to share private information in a public setting.

As Rose walked toward her vehicle, she turned and threw a question back at Debbie.

"What happened to physio, I thought you kept studying while working in London?"

"I did. I'm qualified. But I worked at some of the best coffee shops as a student and decided I just love it. Coffee is my calling," Debbie called out. She pointed to the sign over the cafe entrance that read 'Coffee is my Calling' with a signature across the bottom right corner that Rose instantly recognised: 'Debbie Webb.'

Rose looked at Debbie in awe. "Your own business? I am so impressed!"

"Long story, but the premises had been empty for a while, so I did a deal for cheap rent and Jamie chipped in for the fit-out expense. He is so proud of me..." She blushed and hurried back to the counter where customers were lining up.

Rose sat in her Jeep for a moment before starting it. She was proud of Debbie too. Her own business at twenty-six! Engaged to Jamie Tait. She should have seen that coming, they had been an item on and off during their teens; of course they stayed in touch over the years. Rose felt suddenly left behind.

Rose started the vehicle and pulled out quickly, driving a little too fast on the way back to the farm.

Pulling up at the stables in a small cloud of dust, Rose jumped out of her vehicle, gave Ruff a quick pat and walked through to the round yard where she had left Topper earlier that morning. She opened the gate and walked confidently up to the large grey stallion. She had known this horse since she was young, but her grandfather only let her ride him in later years. He was headstrong and unpredictable.

"Want to go for a gallop old boy?" She slipped her hand

through his halter. Clipping on a lead rope she led him to the edge of the yard, tying him to the fence. Rose looked at her own stock-saddle, then chose her grandfather's heavier western-style saddle. It's what the horse is used to. She threw a clean saddle cloth on first and Topper turned his head and drew his lips back in what looked like a snarl.

"Oh, you're going to be like that are you? Well, be my guest, I feel like a fight." she muttered to the horse as she tightened the girth strap and slipped the crupper around under his tail, doing it up at the back of the saddle. The horse hunched a bit when the crupper went on. He may have a pig-root or buck, but how bad could it be? The horse is seventeen years old.

Selecting his bridle from the tack room, Rose checked the leathers and buckles through habit, then slipped the bit in his mouth. Sliding the rest of the bridle up over his ears, she did the chin strap up quickly. Rose checked the stirrup length and girth tension before she mounted and managed to squeeze it up another notch. "Suck your belly in, old boy, I don't want a loose saddle."

Rose pulled her long hair into a low plait and slapped her old Akubra on her head, before undoing the lead rope from the fence and tying it loosely around his neck. Holding the reins firmly in her left hand, she put her left foot into the stirrup and threw her right leg up and over, settling her backside into the saddle. The seat was a little roomy, but comfortable and well worn.

Topper stood for a moment, quivering. "Deciding whether to buck, are you?" Rose said aloud. He seemed to sense her mood and stepped out as she nudged him with her heels.

"Stay," she said to Ruff as he started to trot after the horse.

As much as she wanted to gallop, she knew Topper was

unfit, so alternated between a quick walk and a trot for the first kilometre while they became used to each other.

Through the first paddock and onto the track that led down to the creek that ran through the bottom corner of the property, Rose loosened the reins and kicked Topper into a canter. Her Akubra flew off, but she glanced back where it lay and left it, to pick up on the way home. The horse was cantering easily, and she felt the tension loosen from her shoulders and neck. Enjoying the fresh air on her face and the horse moving beneath her, Rose knew she could have spent more time at the farm. Should have. She had forgotten how much she loved it here.

Rose looked at the farm paddocks as she cantered past. Most of the fences were standing straight, with good tension in the wires. Not surprising, she thought. Charlie had always been meticulous about maintenance.

A small herd of yearling Herefords stood in one of the paddocks, grazing on hay that had recently been spread out. She frowned. Who had fed the cattle? Neighbours? There was no green feed in the paddocks near the house, but closer to the creek would be better, as they had the right to pump water from the creek to irrigate on the creek flats.

The big horse seemed to eat up the distance with his easy, long-limbed gait, and suddenly the tree line along the banks of the creek was in view. She slowed to a trot and then a walk as she guided the horse through to the edge of the creek. The grass between the trees was green and lush, even the wallabies weren't able to keep it down, she thought. Maybe she should move a few head of young stock into this area. The creek was shallow in places, more so with the drought dragging on, and cattle would be able to get across it to the state forest on the other side, unless she devised some sort of temporary fencing. Worth some thought, however.

Stopping at her favourite spot; a small grassy space open to the edge of the creek and a large flat boulder perfect for sun-baking, she dismounted. She had come here with Debbie on weekends during their school years. Rose smiled to herself; and later with a boyfriend, when she had one. Jamie's older brother Greg had kissed her here for the first time when she was fifteen and he was about seventeen. Then, when she was sixteen, he had caught her swimming in her undies and tee shirt and had tried to jump her. She snorted. He was never going to win that fight. She chuckled at the memory of Greg trying to explain his broken nose to his parents. She had told Charlie what happened, and he had told her she did exactly the right thing. Anytime a boy made a pass at her she should break his nose! She smiled at the memory. Strange that she had been more comfortable telling Charlie than either of her parents at the time.

Once she left home and moved to the city, she had discovered that it could be more pleasant to enjoy the jump than break the nose. She'd had a couple of relationships while studying and then working in Sydney. Until recently Rose had been dating Mark, a journalist. But she couldn't see him coming home to the farm for Christmas. Somehow her relationships never seemed to go beyond nice dinners and (mostly) good sex. Rose just couldn't seem to let anyone in, emotionally. She was starting to think she wasn't the type to get married and raise a family. Too career oriented, perhaps. Yet thinking back to her conversation with Debbie this morning, she knew deep down that was a lie. An excuse to not get too involved. When she ended it with Mark, he told her she was intimidating.

Really? She had looked at him and thought "you need to grow a pair." She wanted the sort of lover Charlie would have called a 'man's man', but they were an endangered species in the city. Even here, all the good ones marry young.

Dismounting, she tied Topper loosely to a tree, away from the rich green grass. "You're too fat old boy, I don't want you to get colic if you get stuck into this green feed. You're sweating like a pig already, so you can't drink from the creek until you cool down a bit."

Rose looked at the clear water running over the rocks. I, on the other hand, may just slip in for a drink and cool off, she thought. The creek was on her land, so no one would disturb her. She quickly pulled her boots, socks and jeans off, then her shirt and tee shirt. In bra and barely there undies, she waded across the rocks and slightly upstream to a swimming hole deep enough to fully submerge.

Rose plunged in to the cool water, went under and came up, shaking droplets from her face and hair. The drought must be affecting the headwaters of the creek too. It wasn't as deep, or as fast flowing, as she remembered.

Floating lazily in the clear water, she considered the conversation about Charlie's will. She was angry and felt betrayed. Why had he done it? Had he been influenced? She had thought he was 'sound of mind' until the end, but perhaps he wasn't and she hadn't been around enough to pick up on it.

There was a sound like a car door in the distance. Rose decided it was just a branch falling on the other side of the creek. Then Topper began to snort and stomp. Rose looked back to where the horse was tied. He was restless. There may be a wild dog around, although they would be more active at night. She moved to where the creek shallowed and stood up, water dripping from her long plait and her underwear; now wet and transparent, walking through the water toward the place she had left her clothes, by the horse.

As she stepped on to the bank of the creek, a man's voice said, "Don't move. Not a muscle."

Angus Hamilton shifted quietly from the shadows beneath the tree, rifle slung over one arm, close to where Topper stood. The horse moved restlessly, stamping and neighing.

Rose lifted her chin and spoke firmly.

"This is my property. I do not permit hunting; I have valuable stock nearby. Leave now and I will not report you for trespassing." She looked Angus straight in the eye, fully aware her underwear was transparent, but too angry at his boldness to cover herself.

"I said stand still!" Angus spoke just as firmly, his voice steely with menace. Her eyes grew wide as he swiftly raised the rifle, cocking it quietly. Before she could move he aimed and shot, just a metre from where she stood, close to the horse. Rose jumped back in shock, then saw the death throes of a very large red-bellied black snake, curling in on itself.

"How? How did you know the snake was there? How could you see it?" Rose picked up her tee-shirt and drew it on, providing some semblance of modesty.

Angus breathed out loudly as he set the gun down, the safety catch on, before moving closer to Topper, giving him a pat on the neck. "I came in through the state forest." He nodded to the tree-line beyond the fence, a short distance away. "Charlie had problems with cattle getting out. The fence here has been cut twice in as many weeks. We moved the young stock back to the dry paddocks, and I have been doing random patrols when I'm in the area, to see if I can find who is responsible, or catch them in the act."

Rose looked at him directly. "But the rifle? Why? Surely you wouldn't shoot anyone, even if they were stealing cattle?"

Nodding, he said. "You are right. I wouldn't shoot anyone, or even threaten them, necessarily. I carry the rifle in case of wild dogs; they have taken a few calves and lambs in the area lately. In daylight too. The drought is making them bold.

"I was checking the fence and saw Topper tied up, knew you would be at the swimming hole. I've used it myself a few times after Charlie brought me here the first time. I was going to head back to my car when Topper became restless. I couldn't see any dogs, so it could only be a snake and I had glimpsed a large red-belly here a few days ago."

Rose looked down at the dead snake between her and the horse, shuddering. "It's a big one, could have been nasty. I'm a long way from the house and don't have a phone with me. So you were protecting me?"

Angus nodded. "Perhaps I was worried about the horse. Topper was tied up and couldn't escape if you had startled it toward him."

Rose snorted. "Me? Startle a snake that large?"

"When I saw you step out of the water, er, in your underwear, as such ... I was a little nervous myself." Angus wanted to smile, willing her to share a moment with him now the danger had passed. Rose was now clad in transparent underwear and a damp t-shirt.

"Very chivalrous of you, thank you Mr Hamilton ... for protecting *my horse*." Rose glared as she looked Angus up and down. Slowly. Deliberately. She swept her eyes over his faded jeans, riding boots and check shirt with only one button done up, showing a tan and lean muscled chest, his abs ending in a 'v' at the top of his jeans.

Picking up her own jeans, Rose pulled them on, then sat to put her socks and boots on. Angus stepped forward, picked the snake up by the tail, hanging it over the branch of a tree. "Charlie said that snakes don't really die until sundown and you should hang them on a fence or tree, just in case."

Rose stood up, bristling. Who is this man? Really? What hold did he have over Charlie? "You forget that Charlie was *my* grandfather. He told me that myth too, many times." Thoughts of Charlie brought unexpected emotion to her voice, so she raised it to hide her rawness. "I don't know how you wangled your way into Charlie's life and I don't know why he made his will ... so complicated. I am prepared to fight you on this. Bloody snake. You probably planted it here!"

She knew she was being unreasonable, but didn't care. Running to Topper, Rose untied him, threw herself up into the saddle and kicked him into a gallop. She looked back once and saw Angus standing in the same spot, watching her.

6

ngus wasn't sure whether to laugh or be angry at Rose. She could hold her own, that's certain. Despite being caught in her underwear, what little there was of it, she was haughty, yet self-contained. He knew she had grown up on the property, would have come across many snakes and maybe killed a few herself, but that red-belly today, it was large and aggressive. He frowned. She had put her pride before her own safety and that of the horse.

Climbing through the fence he heard a noise, something large in the state forest, but not close. The hair on the back of his neck stood up. Turning slowly, he scanned back to the creek, then to the track Rose had taken on the horse. She was still galloping. Damn her. Topper was unfit. He watched for another moment as the horse and rider became smaller in his vision.

Standing quietly, the rifle still casually held in his right hand, he looked back to the creek. Squinting in the glare of the sun off the water, he tried to see if there was movement on the other side. A light rustle. It could have been anything. Kangaroos, wild dogs, a wombat. He stayed completely still another minute or so. It may have been a man. Cattle rustlers perhaps? How long had they been there? Long enough to see Rose get in, and out, of the creek?

Exhaling slowly he began to walk to the clearing a few hundred metres away, where his ute was parked. Sliding in behind the wheel, he wound his window down and took another long slow look along the fence-line. There was no sign anyone had been there, but he couldn't shake the feeling there had been more danger than just the snake.

Shaking his head, he turned the vehicle to drive slowly out of the forest to the main road. He stopped before turning on to the road. On a whim he turned the engine off. In the distance, back in the state forest, he heard the sound of a motorbike. Two cylinders, he could tell by the faint tinny whine it made. Heading in the opposite direction.

There had been someone there.

He needed to tell Rose, to warn her there had been some strange happenings in the last few months in this area. He also wanted to check on Topper. He was a spirited horse, but Rose had ridden him hard. He'd drop by, it would ease his mind.

7

A drenalin pumping through her, Rose slowed to a canter and glanced around for her fallen Akubra on the way. She couldn't see it, but wasn't sure if she was looking in the right area. She had taken little notice when it came off, enjoying the canter, but had expected it to be easy to spot.

Maintaining her pace until she saw the horse paddock and stables ahead, Rose finally allowed the old stallion to slow to a trot, then walk. Only then did she register that Topper was blowing hard and favouring one leg. She swung off and walked the horse, contrite she had ridden him too hard and caused an injury. Her own breathing beginning to steady, Rose walked him into the round yard and tied him to a rail. Gently speaking while she removed the saddle and bridle, she saw Topper had thick white foam around his flanks.

Rose filled a bucket with water, knowing he would have to

cool down before he could drink. She would sponge him down and that may help. Walking back to the horse with the bucket of water, sponge in her back pocket, she saw Angus Hamilton pull up outside the stables. He swung over the fence to the yards effortlessly and was before her in three strides. Rose saw he was white-hot angry. At her? Why?

The bucket still in her hand, Angus grabbed it from her and tipped the water out. He turned on her, "This is an old horse in unfit condition. You have ridden him hard, and he needs to cool before you let him drink. Charlie, *your* grandfather, would have told you this, I know."

Rose drew herself up, snatched the bucket from him and returned to the tap, refilling it. "This is my horse now. I know how to care for him." Furious at his unjustified remarks, she filled the bucket, dropped the sponge from her back pocket into it, walked back to Topper and began sponging him with the tepid water.

Angus had the good grace to look embarrassed. "I saw the bucket, I thought you were giving him a drink. It could have killed him ..."

Rose stiffened. Who did he think he was? She grew up here. She knew how to look after her animals. What right did he have to question her care?

Angus leant back against the fence as she washed Topper down with the wet sponge.

"We need to talk about Charlie's will. What it means for the farm and both of us. I thought you knew, he said he would talk to you ..." Angus hesitated.

Rose turned on him, "I do not wish to discuss my grandfather's will. Not today. Maybe not ever. I just want to ensure I haven't harmed my horse." She breathed deeply, feeling emotion rise to the surface. Anger? Grief at the loss of Charlie? She didn't know. But Angus Hamilton was still a stranger to her and she would be damned if she would cry in front of him. She turned her back, sponging the horse's back and shoulder.

"Rose, I also need to talk to you about the problems Charlie was having here. Fences cut and cattle getting out. Gun shots beyond the stables at night. Just now, leaving the state forest, I heard a motorbike in the distance. It may just be kids using the state forest to ride un-licenced, but I think there may have been someone else at the creek. Over the other side. Watching you. You need to stay safe. Charlie wanted you to be safe."

Hearing the seriousness of his tone, Rose paused, her back still to him, one arm laid across Topper's shoulder.

"I will speak to the police tomorrow, get an idea of what has been going on in the area. I appreciate your concern. I will be cautious," she started to rub the horse again, the realisation that she was, truly, on her own out here, hitting her.

"Good." Angus wanted to say more, but could see he would need to choose a better moment. He vaulted over the fence and slid into his ute, driving slowly out through the gate.

The horse had cooled and Rose refilled the bucket and let him drink, then gave him a feed. She would keep Topper in the yard and check on him later. She had picked up his hooves, no stones that could cause his slight limp. His right front fetlock seemed warm, she may have to call the vet to him yet.

Back in the homestead Rose could see the answering machine blinking. Her grandfather had never bothered to get a mobile phone. She pressed the button and heard a call from Frances Barlow, reminding her of their dinner engagement. She would call her tomorrow.

Feeling a little stiff and sore from the ride, Rose took a long shower, then threw on light cotton capri pants, a cotton shirt buttoned at the front and a pair of sandshoes. After eating a sandwich leftover from the wake, she walked back to the stables to check Topper. It was getting dark. She threw a light on and went out to the yard. She was shocked to see he was laying down.

Frowning, she murmured to him as she drew closer. He lifted his head. Exhausted, poor thing. She should not have ridden home so hard; he wasn't a young horse anymore. Refilling the bucket, she coaxed him to his feet. As he drank deeply, she noticed he was holding his right front hoof off the ground. The fetlock was swollen and hot. Hell.

Pulling her mobile phone from her back pocket, she googled the local vet and called. It was after hours, but they diverted to a service for emergencies. The call service answered, took the details and confirmed the vet would be there inside an hour.

While she waited Rose brushed Topper and remembered the vet. He had gone to school with her father and was well known in the area. David Petersen was a 'big animal' vet and well-liked by the local farmers. She knew her grandfather had always called on him if the horses needed treatment.

It was fully dark when the vet drove up the driveway, stopping beside her own vehicle at the stables. The headlights were shining in her eyes as she walked across to the fence to greet him.

"Dr Petersen," she called out, "Rose Gordon. Over here with Topper." The vet moved from his vehicle, carrying his bag. With the headlights behind him, he seemed taller than she remembered.

He came into full view and vaulted over the fence with his bag. Angus Hamilton. She was stunned.

He glanced at her. "Oh, you mustn't know. I bought Petersen's practice over a year ago when he retired. Dr Angus Hamilton, at your service."

Rose blushed. Angus walked over to Topper and looked in his eyes and mouth, before running his hands down his legs. After a few moments he looked up at Rose.

"It's not your fault Rose. Topper is getting on and has developed degenerative joint disease, similar to arthritis. This leg is particularly bad. I have been treating him for Charlie, but he was riding less and less these last months. I will inject into the joint, and that will give Topper some relief, but he really needs rest and controlled exercise. He may never gallop again, but he should still be able to do cattle work and have a canter."

He treated the horse while she looked on, biting her lip. Topper still seemed without much energy. She thanked Angus when he was finished and asked him to send the bill. "Don't worry" he said "I could never charge for treating Topper." He smiled at her, placing his large hand on her shoulder as he spoke and her stomach seemed to turn over. Tall, good looking, broad shouldered. Charlie would have called him a man's man.

Rose moved closer. Who was this man? Her grandfather had liked him. A lot, as it turns out. She wanted to reach out and touch those big shoulders.

Then she recalled Barlow's words while reading the will that morning. She stepped back, shivering, wrapping her arms around herself.

"I don't know you and I don't understand why Charlie made his will out the way he did, but until I get legal advice, further use of your services will not be required." Rose felt a physical attraction, an invisible pull, but she couldn't get involved with this man. It surprised her that Charlie had fallen for his country boy-next-door façade, but Rose lived in Sydney, she expected the worst of most people, and was often right to be wary. Angus Hamilton was yet to prove himself honest, or not, but she would wait to learn his true colours.

8

He could see her looking at him. Really looking at him. He looked back at her, taking in her light pants and shirt. He could see she wore a bra, but if she had underwear on under those pants, they were not visible. He recalled her spunky attitude earlier in the day, telling him off while wearing practically nothing. She was brazen and tough. He liked her. He had hoped he would. Charlie had talked about her a lot but he had thought the old man was exaggerating about his beloved granddaughter. This girl was the real deal. Strong, a bit arrogant, resilient.

It was clear Rose was struggling with anger over the unexpected contents of the will, but it was mixed with grief too. He wanted to offer comfort, perhaps help her understand. Stepping toward her, he lightly touched her shoulder and for a moment she seemed to lean toward him, before shrugging his hand away and shutting down, emotionally.

So that is how it is, he thought. He would prefer to discuss the will calmly and help her understand what Charlie was feeling and thinking; show her the benefits. It didn't have to be a fight. Shouldn't be a fight. He needed to gain her trust. He owed it to Charlie.

"I understand. However, I would like to treat Topper as he has been my patient for the last couple of years and I know his history. Don't put pride before his health," Angus patted the horse on the shoulder as he spoke.

Rose knew he was right. She hesitated. "Ok. Treat Topper. Thank you."

They looked at each other for a moment, then Angus picked up his vet bag and turned away.

As he walked to his vehicle, he glanced back at Rose. She looked young and uncertain, standing by the fence. When she saw him looking her way she straightened and glared at him defiantly. He nodded to her before climbing into his vehicle, raising one hand from the steering wheel in acknowledgement before driving away.

He knew it would be complicated, the way Charlie had structured his will. But Charlie had known she would have to sell, couldn't manage on her own, and he hadn't wanted the international conglomerate, Rosewood Beef, getting their hands on this property. They had been buying up properties in the area consistently for more than a year. Charlie had thought his will may allow her to keep it going longer, while she sorted out where she wanted to be; in the city or on the land. Angus had been promised Charlie would explain this to her. Perhaps he had been waiting for her to come home again to do it in person. Angus frowned. Damn you Charlie, for not telling her. And damn you for dying, my old friend.

9

F irst thing next morning, Rose sat in front of Sergeant Carroll's desk at the local police station, suddenly aware of how much had been kept from her over the last year.

"Charlie reported three separate incidents of fence cutting in the last five months. Although most of the stock was missed and quickly rounded up - the neighbours were having similar problems and a combined muster of the state forest was organised – each time there were a couple of animals that were never found. They may still roam the forest, you know how dense it is in there and the deep gullies are almost impossible to traverse, but we suspect they were taken and sold, or butchered for food. It is odd, however, as organised cattle rustlers would have cut the fences, guided the cattle into portable yards and had them away on trucks before daybreak. We are struggling with motive. At the moment it's either kids, or someone in the district with an axe to grind," Sergeant Carroll nodded at Rose.

"Did Charlie mention he was having problems with anyone? There were also gunshots at night on more than one occasion. We investigated where he believed the shooters may have been," he sighed, "but not even a tyre track or bullet shell was found. Charlie became more agitated after each incident, and I wondered .... but perhaps it was also due to his heart playing up. We'll never know now."

"No. He didn't. He didn't tell me about the fences being cut. He didn't tell me he heard gunshots at night. There's a lot he didn't tell me." Disturbed by what she had heard, Rose leaned back in her chair.

"I'm sure he made that decision believing there was no point worrying you in Sydney. There was nothing you could have done...."

Before he could continue Rose blurted out angrily, "I could have been here. I could have been here more often. He worried about this alone. He died alone. I should have been here," she wiped a tear away roughly, breathing deeply to regain her composure.

Sergeant Carroll came around the desk and put his hand on Rose's shoulder, gently. He spoke quietly. "He wasn't alone Rose. We turned out for Charlie's musters along with all of his neighbours and anyone from the community who had a horse, motorbike or quad bike. The CWA ladies, led by Jill Tait, have been keeping him in hot casseroles and scones since Vera passed away," he chuckled, "Charlie told me at the last muster, and I quote 'those damn women are always bringing food by. If they're not shoving it down my throat, they're practically poking it up my arse' unquote."

Rose surprised herself by laughing aloud. "Oh my gosh, he used to say that to grandma all the time. She would hit him with a tea towel, then set down another serve of apple pie, 'for his sins' she'd tell him." Smiling wanly, Rose added "and he always ate every last bit. In fact, his diet was probably too rich and caused his heart congestion ... but the stress of these events would have surely contributed." Saddened by the conversation, Rose added, "whoever is behind this ... deliberate harassment, should be locked up .... " Rose sighed and trailed off.

"No argument here Rose. We have attended every time, but found no hard evidence. Charlie's death was a blow to the whole community."

Rose stood, shaking Sergeant Carroll's hand warmly. "Thank you. I will be vigilant and if anything out of the ordinary occurs, I will call you immediately. I appreciate you filling in some of the gaps for me."

He nodded at this. "Do that Rose. Don't take any risks. We still don't know if it's malicious, or just kids. Call here anytime, there is an officer on call at night, even if the station is closed."

Contemplating his words, Rose walked pensively back up the street to look in at Coffee is my Calling. Perhaps Deb will have time for a quick chat. She rolled her shoulders back as she walked; they were sore from her ride yesterday, as were her legs. If Topper is unfit, I am even worse; she thought.

It was just after ten and only one group of older ladies were sitting in, with two people standing at the counter. Rose couldn't see Debbie, but ordered a coffee and sat down while she digested what she had learned. It explained why Angus was there yesterday. His story checked out.

Or did it? Is it Angus that has been cutting fences and letting cattle out? Is that how he has wormed his way into Charlie's confidence, by helping muster them, supposedly patrolling the fences?

Staring into space, Rose jumped when Debbie slid into the seat next to her, with two coffees.

"Sorry, I didn't mean to startle you. I was out the back and heard your voice. I'd rather have a coffee with you than work out my BAS return. The morning rush is over and the yummy Mummy's don't come in for another hour, so I try to do the paperwork while it's quiet."

Smiling, Rose looked at her friend fondly, "I was hoping I would see you, and if you have time, let's chat." She reached across the table and touched her friend's hand.

Debbie looked hard at Rose, clearly concerned. "Have you hurt yourself? You were fine yesterday. I saw your Jeep parked near the police station, you seemed to be walking a little stiffly. Has something happened?"

Rose considered telling Deb about her conversation with Sergeant Carroll, but knew it was a conversation that should be had when she wasn't working. "Rode the old stallion yesterday, he has hurt his leg but I may have come off worse," she picked up her coffee and sipped, raising her eyebrows over the rim of the mug.

"You should know better, that horse is a demon!"

Twenty minutes later they were still talking and even sharing a laugh and Rose felt she could tell Debbie anything, just as they had when they were younger. She leaned forward, about to find out if her friend would have time later for a proper chat, about the will and Angus Hamilton and his relationship with Charlie, when Debbie jumped up, beaming at two tall, denim clad men entering the café. Rose turned and smiled too when she saw it was the Tait brothers.

Jamie put his arm around Debbie and planted a lingering kiss on her lips, making her blush and smile at the same time. The older ladies at the table nearby looked a little shocked.

Jamie grinned at them, "It's all right, we're getting married," and held Debbie's hand up with the ring sparkling in the sunlight.

"Save it for the wedding night, young man," one of them said, but she smiled as she said it.

Jamie looked at Rose, let out a 'yeehaa' before grabbing her up in his arms, spinning her around and hugging her at the same time.

Breathless, Rose pushed him back, laughing. "Stop it, you're making a scene and I have heard that the owner of this café will not hesitate to remove you, should you misbehave!"

At that, the taller brother stepped forward, nodded at Debbie, then put an arm around Rose, giving a light squeeze. "Nice to have you home Rose, but so sorry you have lost Charlie. Let me know if you need a hand over there with anything, happy to help."

"Thanks Greg, I will let you know," Rose smiled cheekily, "I see you have maintained your rugged good looks," indicating his crooked nose.

"Ah, well Rosie my love, you did me a favour when you broke my nose. Apparently I was such a pretty boy at the time that I was fighting the women, and sometimes the blokes, off with a big stick," he said, trying to look serious, "but after you broke my nose, I learned that only a special woman could love me with this face, so I have been searching for just such a lass all these years." He tried to look sad but Rose was having none of it.

"Enjoy your search Greg Tait, as I am told that your few years playing NRL down in the big smoke enhanced your reputation enormously, and didn't I see you on TV with a model on your arm at last year's Dally M event?"

"Yes, well Rosie, my footy days are over and I have come back to the farm to help young Jamie here, as he has been so distracted by the beautiful Debbie that no work gets done, unless I do it."

Jamie gave his brother a friendly punch on the arm and said, "Your bullshit never worked with Rose. Not when she was sixteen, and not now, so save it for your fans, brother."

The four of them were standing together, laughing and chatting, when Angus Hamilton strode in. He took in the smiling group, noticed how comfortable Rose seemed with them, and also saw the taller of the two men with his arm slung loosely around her shoulders. He felt an unexpected surge of annoyance. He knew Greg Tait was an ex-footy player and a bit of a lad with the girls. He didn't like him being so familiar with Rose.

Debbie saw him and said "Angus, your lunch should be ready, just ask Cath at the counter for it."

"Thanks Debbie." He walked over to the counter, took the bag from Cath and paid her quickly. Without glancing at the group again, he stalked out.

Debbie frowned a little. "Something is up with Angus."

"How well do you know him Deb? Angus I mean," Rose asked.

"He came about two years ago and was a locum for Vet Petersen. He bought the practice about nine months later when Petersen retired. He seems well liked by the farmers, and apparently he is single, so a lot of the local girls have been trying to get to know him. He has shown little interest though. Melanie Mitchell is his Vet Nurse, she came back to town about three years ago with a little daughter, Tiffany. She is school age now. I heard Melanie put it around when Angus first got here that she knew him previously, hinted they were an item. Even said she had told him about the locum opportunity with Dr Petersen. I've only heard this since I came back myself, but I have never seen them together outside of the clinic, and you remember how Melanie was at school?"

Rose remembered. She hadn't gotten along with Melanie. Rose had been a tomboy and with Debbie often hung out with the boys in their grade, playing sport at lunch time. Melanie was one of the popular girls; sporting the latest hairstyle, listening to pop songs and watching the boys play sport. As school progressed, they had no longer been in the same classes, much to Rose's relief.

Debbie was still talking about Angus. "He supports everything in town and is always happy to help folks out. I heard he will even take stock as payment, if any farmer has a cash flow problem. Actually Rose, I think he keeps his stock out at your place, he was close to Charlie. But you probably know that."

"Yep. He has stock at Barrington, that's true. Listen, it was great seeing you all and I'm looking forward to Saturday night at yours for the engagement party. What can I bring?" Rose smiled at the three of them as she turned to leave.

"Boys, take a seat, I need to talk to my girl here," said Debbie, stepping out of the café with Rose. "Actually Rose, I have been hoping to speak to you about this. There is something you can do for me for the engagement."

"Anything Deb," Rose said, wondering what she needed.

"Agree to be my Maid of Honour. Please Rose." Debbie smiled at her friend and held both her hands in hers. "We talked about being each other's bridesmaid when we were kids, and to be honest, it's one of the things I had put off, hoping that we would catch up once I came back from London and you were home at some stage. I didn't expect it to be in these circumstances, but I would love to announce the bridal party on Saturday night. The wedding is not until later in the year, so plenty of time for planning."

It surprised Rose. After barely speaking for the last couple of years the request seemed sudden. But then she thought of the couple of quick catch ups in the last two days, and realised their friendship was still strong, if more mature.

"I'd love to stand up with you at your wedding Deb and happy for you to announce it at the party on Saturday night. So if that's the case, why don't we have a 'girl's night' at my place beforehand, just like old times, and we can talk weddings." Rose hugged her friend, feeling tears well in her eyes. Maybe she wasn't alone. Perhaps she still had a family, of sorts, right here.

Debbie hugged her back and wiped her own eyes with the back of her hand. "This means a lot to me Rose, thank you. Wednesday night will work best." She gave Rose a quick hug, then rushed back behind the counter, as more people had come in while they were chatting.

Rose waved to Debbie and nodded at Jamie and Greg before walking back to her car. She drove home feeling pensive. She still had the invitation to dinner that night with Douglas and Frances Barlow. She needed to discuss Charlie's state of mind with them. She wanted to find out what they knew about Angus and his relationship with Charlie.

Back at the farm, Rose picked out a bottle of wine to take to dinner and left it on the kitchen counter, before heading down to the stables to check on Topper, Ruff trotting beside her. She climbed into the yard and gave him a brisk rubdown. The swelling had gone down in his leg and he seemed content. She decided he was well enough to return to the horse paddock with the two mares and the young filly.

She opened the gate and walked into the paddock, Topper walking behind her, nudging her with his head. She smiled and patted him, hugging his neck. "Here you are, with all your girl-friends to take care of." He trotted into the paddock and rounded up the mares, putting them into one corner. Rose sighed as she saw the mares nicker to him and touch noses.

She looked across at the young filly. Only about two years old, Charlie had told her on the phone he had been working her in the round yard, getting her used to the bit and the bridle. She looked spirited, a dark grey with black mane and tail. Rose knew she was a daughter of Topper. She wondered if she would have time to keep working the young horse, break her to saddle. Coming down only once a month or so wouldn't be enough.

10

Sitting at the beautifully set table with Frances and Douglas Barlow, dinner almost over, Rose smiled sadly at them both.

"So he was definitely of sound mind when he made the will," Rose stated, seeing their nods to confirm.

"And you don't know why he included Angus Hamilton in the will?"

Frances Barlow put her hand gently on Rose's shoulder, as she cleared the remains of their dinner away. "We know Charlie liked and respected Angus. They spent a lot of time together. He never discussed it, but it seemed like Charlie felt he owed Angus a debt of some kind."

"Rose, when your grandfather asked me to draw up a new will in this way, I questioned him and was frankly, quite reluctant. When he told me he would get another lawyer to do it if I wouldn't, I relented. I felt it would be easier for you to deal with us, my dear," Douglas said in his quiet, deliberate manner. "My only thoughts are that Charlie felt you may have a better chance of hanging on to the property if he did this. I know he felt you would have to sell, and he was trying to avoid that."

"It still doesn't make sense. The house and land are mine, and the few horses, but Angus Hamilton owns the stock. Over three hundred head of prime beef. The cattle are worth as much on the hoof as the land itself. If it was that simple, I could make him move his stock from my land, but he also has a lease on the land, for three years, to run the stock. Not just the land, but the plant and equipment as well. OK. I understand that the monthly lease payments will provide enough income for me to maintain the homestead and the horses. But I can't sell, even if I wanted to, while he has the leasehold. So that's three years.

"And not only that, does he really have the right to move into the homestead? It is mine after all." Rose's voice rose slightly, giving way to frustration.

Frances looked at her husband, then sat down next to Rose. "I think Charlie believed the house needs to be lived in Rose. You have your apartment and life in Sydney and Charlie did not want you to change your plans, your dreams, to please him. If you only visit once a month or so, the house will soon fall into disrepair. It is a beautiful old homestead and needs to be maintained. As it is, you will need to engage a gardener with some regularity.

"Charlie said something that surprised me a little, while we were doing his will. He said that he had forced your father to stay on the farm. That Jim would still be here if he had given him a choice. I never heard Jim mention that he wanted to do anything other than farming, but perhaps there was a time he wanted to leave," Frances added.

An old memory hit Rose; she could not have been more

than ten or eleven. She had wandered into her father's little study. It was filled with books. She was looking for information on World War Two for a school assignment. As she was browsing the shelves, her father had walked in. She had looked at him and asked "why do you have so many books on war and aeroplanes Dad?" He had looked a little sad as he answered, "I wanted to be a pilot when I was young, about your age. I've always been interested in planes and flying." Rose had responded with a request for help to find information for her assignment and had never thought about the brief conversation again. Until now.

Frances was still discussing how Rose may share the homestead with Angus, as allowed in Charlie's Will. "Perhaps you can speak to Angus about it. Work out a schedule. He has an apartment of sorts at the back of the Vet clinic where he lives now. He may be happy to stay there when you are home, and at the homestead when you are away."

Rose looked at Frances. "Yes, he may do. It's only for three years and I guess it gives me time to find my feet, decide to keep it or sell it. I could get him to move the cattle after the lease runs out and restock it myself if I sell my apartment in Sydney. Did you know I bought that from the proceeds of Mum and Dad's wills?"

Douglas smiled at Rose. "Good. Be pragmatic, not emotional. Think this through. There is an upside. While I don't know why Charlie made this arrangement with Angus, it may work out OK for you and give you some thinking space. Think on it tonight and try to make a time to speak further with Angus. We can do it here, if you like," Douglas offered.

"Thank you both." Rose impulsively hugged them. "I knew you would be voices of reason. I will 'put my big girl pants on', as they say, and call Angus tomorrow and ask him to have lunch at the homestead with me. I will be civil, businesslike, pragmatic," she smiled at Douglas "and will serve up one of the fabulous casseroles Jill Tait left in the fridge for me. I think it will be better if I tackle this on my own, although I thank you for your advice."

"While talking about the farm. Were you aware that someone had been cutting fences in properties bordering the state forest, letting valuable stock loose? Wild dogs picked off a few young ones before they could be mustered. Cattle rustlers would move them overnight, so why, and who, would be so cavalier?" Rose looked expectantly at them both.

Douglas spoke. "No one knows Rose. You're right, it can't be cattle rustlers. Some say kids. Town kids that don't understand the value of the stock. Others say that it's a tactic used by Rosewood Beef, who are buying up land around here, but that doesn't seem likely either. The consortium is international, big business. They wouldn't have time, or appetite, for such carry on.

"Charlie, however, was dead against the consortium. They made several offers for Barrington, very good offers. But Charlie wasn't interested, wouldn't even discuss the option. With the drought heading well in to its third year, your place is the jewel in the crown. It is one of the few that has permanent water and the right to irrigate. If the consortium had your place, it could provide water for the dry blocks they have already acquired. Charlie worried they would cut others off from the flow on if they had control of the headwaters."

Driving home, Rose thought through her options. Yes, she would definitely invite Angus for lunch tomorrow if he was free, and try to work out an amicable arrangement to share the property the way her grandfather had intended. She yawned as she turned into the driveway; it was late, and she had been up since dawn.

She frowned when she saw a strange car in front of the homestead. It was a souped-up Commodore, mag wheels, very showy. Rose slowly got out of her own car and walked toward the house. Ruff came to meet her and nudged her hand with his nose. She patted the dog quickly and continued warily up the path, between the roses, to the front steps. A large male shape stood up and lurched toward her from the depths of the veranda.

Rose screamed and jumped back.

"Iss only me Rosie, your old pal Greg from next door." Rosie could now see Greg Tait standing by her front door, beer in hand, clearly drunk.

Her heart thumping, Rose spoke firmly. "Greg. You're drunk and you frightened me. What are you doing here?"

Rose started up the steps toward him.

Greg grabbed her by the waist and swung her around, pulling her close to his chest. "Rosie, you know I've always fancied you. You were the only girl in town that didn't chase after me. I've always wanted you."

Ruff growled at Greg. Rose pulled back and slapped his hands away. Wary now. He was a big bloke.

"Greg, Stop it! You're drunk. I'm not interested. Step back!"

"You don't know what you're missing Rosie, I'm damn good in the sack. We'd be great together, just come over here and I'll show you." He lurched toward her, Rose stepped to one side and Greg staggered down the stairs into the rosebushes.

Damn, she thought. I must get him up and inside. He will need cleaning up and sobering up, I can't let him drive like that.

She opened the front door, then went down the stairs and helped him out of the roses. He offered her a drink from his beer. Rose took it and promptly tipped it out into the garden.

"Aaaw, Rosie..."

"Get inside Greg." Rose was firm. "I'll make you a coffee and help you clean up." She draped one of his arms across her shoulders and put hers around his waist, helping him up the stairs and into the house. She took him through to Charlie's study, there was a comfy old couch in one corner. Sitting him down, she started to unwrap his arm from her shoulder, but he grabbed her hard and pulled her onto his lap. He had one hand on her breast and his mouth all over hers, still drunk, but aware of his actions.

With a surge of anger-fuelled adrenalin Rose pushed herself off Greg's lap and swung upward with her right fist, connecting him hard just below the eye. He let go, stunned.

"Just stop it Greg! I was going to let you sleep it off here, but I can just as easily call your mother to come and get you. I am sure she would be very proud to see her football star son in this state." Rose glared at him.

Greg looked away. He was sobering up. "I'm sorry Rosie, it seemed like a good idea at the pub. I'll behave. Let me stay. Don't upset Mum."

"Ok. You're on notice. I'm making you coffee and getting the first aid kit. You can tend yourself, I'm going to bed. My door will be locked." Rose quickly made a coffee, bringing the first aid kit in with it, leaving it on a small table beside the couch. Greg was already sprawled across the couch, asleep. It looked like he would have a black eye. Good luck explaining that to your Mum, she thought.

Rose went to her room and locked the door, then opened it

again and called Ruff in from the veranda. She laid a blanket on the floor beside her bed for the old dog. She was not taking chances. Greg had obviously had an easy time with girls in his football days. Well, she wasn't one of them, and really had no interest in him at all. Jamie was the pick of the brothers, but Debbie had claimed him when they were young, so Rose had never gone there.

11

ngus drove up the driveway quietly just before dawn, intending to check on the old stallion before he started his morning small animal clinic in town. He saw the Commodore in front of the homestead as he went past and knew it belonged to Greg Tait. It must have been there all night, he thought, his stomach clenching at the thought of Rose with Tait. Well, they had seemed very familiar yesterday at the cafe, perhaps he was an old boyfriend. She was a grown woman. A woman of passion, he thought. She could have a local lover. Irrationally, he hated the thought; tried to ignore it as he pulled up by the stables. Had he expected her to like him on sight, just because Charlie thought they would get on?

He found the stallion out in the paddock with the herd and brought him in. He checked him over, but he still looked lethargic, although his leg had settled down. Damn old age, he thought. First Charlie, now Topper was looking poorly. He would come back later with a tonic and some molasses, that may perk him up a bit.

He should leave a note at the house for Rose, letting her know he had brought the horse into the yard. He stopped his car beside the Commodore. As he walked up the front steps the door opened and Greg stood there, just in jeans, a towel in his hand.

"Angus. Good morning, you're early for a house visit? Rose is still asleep. Would you like me to wake her?" Greg looked confident and comfortable, standing at the door of the homestead.

Angus shook Greg's hand quickly and noted the swelling around his eye. He handed him the note, "Just leave this for Rose, I've brought the stallion in and will drop back later to look in on him. He is not doing well."

Greg looked at the note and nodded to Angus, "Sure. I will let her know."

Angus departed and Greg looked at the note, then shoved it in his pocket. He knew he had handled Rose badly last night, he would have to use a little more finesse and charm. Not only did he really fancy her, but she now owned one of the best farms in the district. He could get on board with that. What's not to love? He needed to make himself indispensable to her, that was the trick.

He went back into the house and quietly tidied up the couch, removing all signs he had been there. He went down the steps to the rose garden and cut three beautiful blooms, bringing them back in to a vase on the kitchen bench. He went into Charlie's study and wrote a note to Rose, apologising for last night. Then he walked out the door and slid into his car. He was about to start up, but then got out, hurried down to the stables and let the old stallion out into the horse paddock.

12

R ose woke to the sound of Greg's V8 engine heading slowly up the drive toward the main road. What a night, she thought. Her right hand was sore, her knuckles swollen. Not broken though, she thought. Only back a few days and she had slugged a man. Damn, being home turned her into a street fighter.

She padded around the house in a long tee shirt and undies, while she checked if Greg had left a mess. She was pleasantly surprised he had tidied up, then she saw the roses and the note of apology in the kitchen. Nice one Greg, she thought, but still no golden ticket for you, buddy. She breathed in the fragrance of the roses; the scent reminding her strongly of her grandmother.

After a quick shower and breakfast, Rose spent the morning in Charlie's study. She wanted to sort through his paperwork, check if any bills needed paying and also email her office and ask for a further week off.

Her boss was OK with the extended leave, but had sent her a new manuscript to edit. Rose had a quick look. Oh crap, another quickly written, poorly plotted manuscript. Sometimes her job sucks. Where are all the decent books, stories with depth and real characters? Damn, she could write a better story herself.

After three hours in the study, with Charlie's paperwork largely sorted, Rose took a break. Then she remembered she had been going to call Angus and invite him for lunch. Maybe she would make it tomorrow, instead. She strolled through the house and out the front door, whistling Ruff as she went. She walked down to the stables and hauled a small bale of hay out into the yard, opened the gate into the horse paddock and called the horses up. After a few minutes the two mares appeared, and the filly, so she spread the hay out for them while she waited for the stallion.

He didn't appear and Rose felt anxious; it was unlike Topper not to come up for hay with the mares. She walked further into the paddock; it dropped off on one side to a stand of native gum trees, and beyond that a small grassy spot where the horses liked to graze. Coming through the trees she saw the stallion. He was down, flat on his side.

Oh no, she thought, he's dead! She ran to him, found him breathing shallowly. She got his head up and brought his back legs in under him to try to rock him to his feet or at least a sitting up position. He just didn't have the strength, and she started crying, "don't die now Topper, please don't die." She thought of running back to the house to call the vet, call Angus, but didn't want to leave the horse.

Greg found her there an hour later. He had returned to apologise in person and when Rose didn't answer his knock, although her car was there, knew she would be with the horses.

Walking up to her, he lifted her to her feet and just held her for a moment. Rose sobbed on his chest briefly before stepping back.

"Can you go and call the Vet please Greg? Call Angus. He knows Topper. He can help. I can't leave him, please call Angus," Rose pleaded.

Greg looked fondly at Rose for a moment before nodding. He returned minutes later, a rifle slung over his arm. Rose looked at him in horror.

"No!" she screamed. "You will not shoot this horse! No. Did you call Angus? Did you even bloody call Angus?" Rose shoved Greg away, but he was much bigger, and sober today.

He held her firmly by the shoulders. "The horse needs to be put down. It's kinder. He won't ever be any good now. One quick shot. I'll do it for you Rose. Walk up to the stables, I'll put the old bugger out of his pain, then I'll dig a hole and bury him down the bottom of this paddock. You're a farm girl, you know I'm right." Greg inserted a bullet into the rifle, before snapping it shut and stepping over to where the horse lay.

Rose screamed again and threw herself down beside Topper, cradling his head in her arms.

At that moment Angus burst through the trees at a run. He had seen Tait's car by the stables and heard Rose scream and shout. He wasn't sure what he would find, but Topper flat on the ground, Rose protecting him with her own body, and Tait stalking about with a cocked rifle was not what he expected.

Greg swung around, facing Angus, the rifle still in his hands. Angus stopped and studied him for a moment. They were similar in build, Angus maybe one or two years older. Rose, relieved to see Angus, called out.

"Leave Greg. Now! Take your bloody rifle and piss off! If Topper needs to be put down, Angus will do it. Gently. You are not shooting this horse."

Angus looked at Greg. He noted several expressions cross his face and his stance stiffen; the rifle raised higher. Without speaking, Angus, vet bag in hand, stepped around Greg to Rose and the horse.

Greg hesitated for a moment. "I was trying to help you Rose. The last thing I want to do is shoot old Topper, but you can see he is in pain. I will check on you later." He walked back through the trees toward the stables, disappearing from sight. Minutes later a large flock of galahs rose from the gumtree by the stables as the Commodore exited loudly toward the road.

Angus lifted Rose to her feet. He considered berating her for letting the horse out, it would have been easier to treat him in the yard, but given the events of the last few minutes said nothing as he began to check the animal over.

"He's not good Rose. If we can get him to his feet, we might be able to get him back to the stables, but frankly, I don't think he has the energy."

"It's my fault, I rode him too hard, it's all my fault." Rose shook her head, close to tears again, as she stroked the old horse's cheek. Angus sighed before speaking.

"It would have been easier if you had left him in the yard this morning. I was coming back to treat him, although he could have gone down there too."

"Left him in the stables? He was out here when I got up, he didn't come when I called and I came down here and found him like this. He wasn't in the yards; the gate was open." She looked at Angus in confusion.

Angus thought back, he was sure he had closed the gate from the yard to the paddock. It was still only half light, maybe he didn't latch it properly.

"I'll give him a shot, see if we can get him on his feet. Otherwise ..."

Rose looked at him sadly. "No. You can't put him down without trying. You have to try. Please try." She gulped noisily.

Angus filled a syringe and injected the horse in the loose flesh of his neck and waited. Nothing happened for a few minutes, then the stallion lifted his head and tried to get his legs under him.

"Quick Rose, push his back legs under, I'll take his front. Together they rocked the horse into a sitting position. Rose came back around to the stallion's head and held it in her hands. "Please Topper, we have to get you up. Please. Do it for me. Do it for Charlie."

Angus waited while she coaxed the horse, speaking soothingly to him as she stroked his nose, his neck. Suddenly the stallion rocked himself over his feet and stood up, quivering.

"All right Rose, hold his headstall and walk him up slowly. Stop if he needs to."

Together they got back to the yards, then took him through to a stall in the stables. Rose forked fresh hay onto the floor and put a little grain and molasses in his food bin, and water in the trough, while Angus worked on him.

Angus looked at Rose with concern. "We may just be delaying the inevitable Rose, you have to consider Topper and the discomfort he is in. He is getting worse, I'm sorry."

Rose stepped back from Angus, shaking her head. "No. No. Give him some time, he needs more time!"

In a whisper, almost to herself, she added, "I've lost every-one, everything. Not this horse too. I need this horse."

Angus sighed, nodded and turned back to Topper. "We can make him comfortable. If we can get him to eat a little of the molasses mixture, he may pick up. I don't want him to go down again, as I am afraid he won't get up if he does."

Rose held the molasses mixture under Topper's nose, willing him to eat. The horse sniffed at it and snorted, sending little pieces of chaff flying off Rose's hand. Trying not to cry, she gently pushed the mixture against his mouth.

With her back to Angus, Rose leant against the horse. "I will stay with him. I don't want him to be alone. If he is going to die, I will be here."

Angus looked at her back for a long moment, noting the slump in her shoulders and the tone of resignation in her voice. "All right Rose," he said quietly, "I will come back early this evening. Stay with him."

13

Ngus attended his call outs, including a stud bull torn badly on a barbwire fence, chasing a neighbour's heifer. It was almost dark when he drove to Barrington. He saw lights on at the stables and knew he would find Rose there with the horse.

He had wondered, after being greeted by Greg at the door in the early morning, if Rose was involved with him. Did she sleep with him, as Greg hinted? Seeing her anger at the man later in the morning slightly allayed his fears in that direction. Maybe she had slept with him. Maybe she hadn't, but her angry demand that he 'piss off' didn't hint at overtones of affection. Good.

He walked in to the stall. Rose heard him and gave him a small smile. "He seems better. He has been drinking and ate a mouthful of the feed."

Angus nodded at her and stepped up to Topper, running his hands over him. He stepped back and looked at Rose. "He looks brighter. If we can get him through tonight, he has a good chance. I will give him another tonic, it will take around thirty minutes to take effect." Angus prepared an infusion and administered it while Rose held the horse quietly.

Angus touched Rose on the arm gently, "Come out here, we can watch him while we have dinner."

"Dinner?" Rose blinked in surprise.

"Dinner. You won't have eaten anything since breakfast. I know you haven't left Topper all day. I picked up a couple of sandwiches from Debbie's on the way out here."

Angus lifted a small esky onto a hay bale outside the stall, offering Rose a ginger beer and a wrapped sandwich. Rose hesitated, then looked at him gratefully. "Actually, I'm starving. Thank you."

They perched up on the hay bale with the makeshift picnic between them. They talked quietly while they ate, watching the old horse move around the stall. Angus told Rose about the emergency with Kenneth Rowland's stud bull earlier that day, and made her chuckle as he described how Kenneth wanted to personally check the bull's testicles were not injured, and the nasty kick to the hip he got for his trouble.

Angus saw Rose relax as he spoke about his work. He had a genuine passion for his vet practice and was getting to know the town and locals well. She was watching his face, seeming to enjoy the sound of his voice, when he suddenly stopped and leant forward. Rose quickly turned toward the stall, heart thumping, to see Topper with his head in the feed bin, eating noisily. She laughed out loud and turned back to Angus, grinning broadly, "you can't keep a good horse down. Look at that, surely that's a good sign?"

He smiled back and stood up. Standing side by side they

leaned over the door of the stall watching the horse eat until he pulled his head out and nickered to them.

Angus looked down at Rose. How happy she was to see the old horse pick up. "Top up his water Rose but don't give him any more feed until morning. Why don't you get some rest and I will meet you back here early tomorrow?"

Rose looked unsure.

"He is eating Rose. A dying horse doesn't eat. You may have to watch him closely for a few more days, but tomorrow you can let him out into the yard and walk him. If he continues to improve, you can let him back in with the mares the next day. One day at a time."

"OK, thank you Angus. Thank you for this," she gestured to the horse, "and thank you for saving me from that snake two days ago. I am grateful you were there." She looked him in the eyes, showing the sincerity of her words.

As she spoke, however, he saw a shadow cross her face. She hesitated before asking, "Why were you there? Really? Checking the fences …. Or cutting them?"

Angus paused, his jaw seemed to clench. "Is that what you think Rose? That I would cause you the same grief that probably hastened Charlie's death?"

Deliberately relaxing his jaw, he added, "There is something or someone creating mischief for local farmers and I have my suspicions but no evidence. I wanted to warn you about the goings on out here, was worried about you being here by yourself. I planned to on the day of the funeral. I was hoping to speak to you after the wake, but you gave me short shift, which I deserved, so I said nothing." He looked away.

It was Rose's turn to look embarrassed. "I didn't know who you were Angus. I now remember my grandfather speaking warmly of you, but in my mind you were a friend, someone his own age, that he was spending time with. I had no notion of his will or that I would lose him. He had not told me about the fence cutting either, or the campaign by Rosewood Beef to sell out. I was rude to you that day. I have no excuse."

Angus moved closer and put an arm across her shoulders, squeezing gently. "I was feeling raw too, Rose. I had just lost a dear friend. You lost your only family. Neither of us was prepared."

Rose leant in to his embrace slightly, then pulled away. "Angus, we need to talk about the will and how to proceed."

"Yes. Good. Thank you." Angus looked at the horse again and nodded to Rose. "Tomorrow morning at 6am to visit my patient. We will make a time to talk properly."

14

Rose woke to the shrill tone of the house phone. She had been dreaming about a fire and in her dream the fire engines were screaming toward her.

Shaking her head, she padded out to the kitchen, feet bare. The sun was rising, sending fingers of gold through the kitchen window, creeping along to the fruit bowl on the big oak table. The phone stopped before she could pick up. Rose was about to dial last number when it rang again.

"Rose Gordon."

"Rose. It's Jill Tait. Someone's cut your fence and ours in the night. We have cattle in the state forest, more of ours than yours, I think. Are you able to meet us at Woolshed Lane in sixty minutes? We are gathering a group to muster them out from there. The boys have gone in on bikes already, Ross is on a quad, but I am hoping you can come on horseback, the bikes can't go everywhere.

"Neale Campbell and his sons are setting up a portable

yard, so we can sort them when we flush them out. Campbell's younger son and daughter are standing by the breaks in the fence, so no more get out. We'll put them back through the same way, then Jamie and Greg can repair the fences." Pausing a moment, Jill added, "If Ross and the boys catch the little bastards they will have their backsides kicked."

"You think it's kids, Jill?" Rose asked.

"It has to be. There is no other explanation."

"I may be longer than sixty minutes, I will saddle Calico, the stock horse mare I usually ride when I'm home. She's good with cattle and doesn't mind the noise of bikes. I'll bring Ruff."

"Good, yes, bring Ruff. See you soon." Jill hung up.

Rose ran back to her room, throwing on jeans and tee shirt, biting into an apple as she pulled on her riding boots. Whistling Ruff, she ran to the stables. Topper was quietly eating, she noted happily. She threw a bale of hay into the round yard and whistled the horses. Moments later the two mares and filly appeared, pleased for an unexpected early morning feed.

Back in the tack room, Rose selected Calico's bridle and saddle, checking them quickly as she did. She was saddled up and just tightening the girth as Angus drove in. Rose remembered he was coming at six to check on Topper.

She called out as he got out of the car. "Topper looks good. Eaten most of the feed. I've topped up his water."

"Jill Tait called. Fences cut again. Young stock in forest. Tait boys have gone in on bikes. Need horses too. I'm heading there now. Taking Ruff." Rose knew she was speaking in shorthand, heard Angus swear at the news, but had no time to add details.

"Where are you meeting? Woolshed Lane?" Angus called.

Rose nodded as she mounted Calico. The stock horse responded to her touch, seemed eager to be away.

Whistling to Ruff, Rose patted the saddle in front while extending her left foot in its stirrup. The old dog leapt up, using her foot as leverage to reach the saddle in front of her, where he settled, leaning back against Rose. Arms around Ruff and reins firmly in hand, she nodded at Angus's obvious surprise, while a gentle kick sent the mare into a canter, the old dog happily lolling his tongue out in the light breeze.

Cutting across her front paddocks, almost bare of grass, only stopping to open and close two gates, Rose arrived at the Woolshed Lane meeting place fifty minutes after taking Jill's call.

Jill smiled and waved Rose over. Rose trotted the mare to where she stood, Ruff leapt down from his perch and gave Jill's hand a lick. She patted his head while handing Rose a small thermos.

"Coffee. Black and strong. I know I woke you and you won't have eaten," Jill started to move to the back of her Landcruiser. The tailgate was down, she had a large thermos and an array of sandwiches and cakes set up.

Rose took a sip. Black and very strong. "I grabbed an apple Jill, thanks. The coffee is great. I'll eat when we get back with the first mob." Rose handed the thermos back to Jill. "Which direction did the boys go? Do you know where they want me to head?"

"They've gone through to the old logging camp, it's about the only place with green grass. We think most of them will go there. But there's always some that head into that gully to the right, it runs down behind your place on the other side of the creek. You and Ruff can head that way, flush any you find out from in there. The bottom of the gully still has feed, so if they find it they won't be keen to leave."

"OK." Rose turned her mare and trotted into the forest, Ruff loping behind. She veered to the right and after a few hundred metres, saw where the gully started, heavily wooded. Slowing to a fast walk, Rose scanned the ground before her. She could see hoof marks and small saplings bent over and trampled in some places. The trees were too thick to move fast, and she wasn't keen to surprise the cattle from behind, which would only push them further into the thick undergrowth.

Ruff stopped, growled at one point, his hackles rising. Rose stood in the stirrups, trying to see if he was growling at cattle, or perhaps wild dogs. The dog was looking up and to the right, still growling. Rose followed his gaze, drew a breath when she saw a huge diamond python draped across a low-lying branch.

"Come on Ruff, that one won't hurt us." She moved past the spot where the snake was. Pythons didn't really worry her. Non-venomous and slow moving after a feed, the snake was no threat.

Pushing on, she could hear the faint sound of motorbikes and shouting to the left, some distance away. It sounded liked the boys may have found most of the cattle and were pushing them back to the temporary yards at Woolshed Lane. Rose had noted Neale Campbell had started setting up the yards. They had a few small bales of hay to give the cattle when they got there, which would help settle them before drafting them into two or more mobs and guiding them back to their respective paddocks.

Ruff gave two short barks. Rose stopped. She could see the dark red coat of a young Hereford through the trees, and could hear more of them moving around.

She turned off the rough track the cattle had made, forging a way through the trees and thick undergrowth to go around them, get in front and start pushing them back the way they came. About twenty metres further on, Rose saw where the gully descended quickly, and deeply. If the cattle got down there, it would be impossible to get them back. She wouldn't like to take a horse down, it looked treacherous. She continued walking the mare steadily through the trees and scrub until she saw the small clearing, still with green feed, and eight fat yearlings grazing.

Whistling Ruff, she entered the clearing. Lifting their heads, the cattle saw Ruff and the stock horse and started trampling back up the path they had used to get down to the gully. With the scrub so thick, they had to stay bunched. Heading in the right direction, Ruff trotted back and forth behind them, occasionally giving a happy little yap to remind them he was there.

Rose didn't have to give the old dog much direction, he knew what to do. Calico was the same, she moved along steadily behind the cattle, turning one way, then the other, if a beast started to veer. The horse moved before Rose could use hands or knees for guidance. Got to love a well-educated stock horse, she thought to herself.

Another thirty minutes and the trees began to thin. Rose could hear activity, voices and bikes, where the yards were set up. Knowing she would see them shortly, she let out a long whistle, so those at the yards could watch out for the stock she was bringing in.

The vista opened up, Rose could see the yards, cattle and her neighbours a few hundred metres away. The cattle saw them too and picked up speed. Six headed straight toward the yards and the hay, but two were spooked. They took off to the left, toward the junction of Woolshed Lane and Barrington Road, which was a busy main road. Rose nudged Calico from trot to gallop without hesitation, heading around the yearlings, turning just before the highway. Calico propped, and the beasts turned again, heading back toward the forest.

Rose galloped along the right side of them, wheeling them to the left. The cattle slowed slightly, turned and seemingly defeated trotted toward the yard and their fellow escapees, their sides heaving. Slowing to a canter, Rose lifted one hand from the reins to wipe her forehead, sweating in the early sun, although it was not yet eight o'clock.

At that moment, a motorbike shot out from the trees beside her, behind a lone beast, bigger than the yearlings, heading toward her on the horse. The motorbike overtook the animal and turned it, but not before Calico, startled, had bucked. With only one hand on the reins, Rose almost lost her seat, but by clamping her knees and sitting deep in the saddle, she stayed on while the mare bucked once or twice, before stopping, shuddering slightly. Rose let the mare stand for a moment, leaning forward in the saddle to pat her on the neck while speaking soothingly.

Crisis over, she walked the mare toward the group by the yards, noticing that Angus was there, in the yard with the cattle, helping to sort them. Feeling exhilarated by the unexpected cattle-work, Rose dismounted as those standing around clapped their hands.

Ruff appeared beside her, nudging her leg. She knelt down and buried her face in his fur, her arms around the old dog, feeling suddenly emotional, yet triumphant. "Thank you old friend, good work."

Ross Tait stepped over, taking the mare's reins in one hand, resting his other on her shoulder for a moment. "Grab a cuppa and something to eat love. I'll give Calico some water and hay." Rose smiled her thanks, as his large hand lingered on her shoulder for a moment, "You did well love. Charlie would be proud."

Taking a drink of water first, Rose reached for a sandwich as she realised how hungry she was. She poured some water into a plastic bowl for Ruff, who drank thirstily then promptly curled up in the shade of the Landcruiser. The men in the yards had two young dogs with them, sorting the cattle into two mobs, but Ruff seemed to know he had done enough for the day.

Rose chatted with Jill for a moment, then walked with her to lean on the fence where they watched the men walking between the cattle quietly, not wishing to stir them up, the dogs following spoken directions, whistles and hand gestures.

Greg came alongside the fence, concern on his face. "You OK Rose? Thought you might lose your seat when I chased that steer out. Big bugger. Probably been in 'ere for months but we missed it last few times we mustered."

Rose chuckled. "Wasn't sure I'd hang on either. It was quite a ride through the scrub. Think I'll be sore tomorrow."

She watched Greg as he climbed over the fence and moved effortlessly among the beasts milling in the yards. Perhaps he wasn't such a bad bloke. Sober anyway.

Glancing over at Angus working with the smaller mob now they had sorted them into two groups, she saw him looking at her. Their eyes met for a moment above the backs of the constantly moving animals. Something in his gaze made her stare, somewhat defiantly at him for a moment, before turning back to respond to a question from Jill.

"Do you need help to get yours back through to your place?

Neale's daughter, Freddie is still there by the cut fence, she will help and I know Angus will give you a hand. He says he can mend the fence once you get them through, too." Jill smiled as Ruff rose from his nap and trotted over to sit by Rose's feet.

"Charlie used to say that Ruff understood every word he said. I'm beginning to believe him. It looks like his nap is over and he is ready to help you walk the herd home. What with Ruff and Calico, you probably could manage on your own."

Rose had a hand on Ruff's head as she nodded at Jill's words. He was an extraordinary dog, that's true. The last cattle dog Charlie trained. Loyal and smart. Although he appeared to have readily transferred his loyalty to Rose, seeming to understand that Charlie was not coming back.

Jill continued, more softly, moving closer to Rose as she spoke. "You know Ruff was with Charlie when he died? It seems he had a stroke in the very early hours. He had stepped outside for some reason. Died right there on the veranda. Angus found him at dawn, Ruff sitting beside him. Angus had been coming in to feed the horses and take hay to the young stock before he started his rounds, as Charlie had been poorly for a week or so. I think it was an excuse for Angus to check on him too. They were pretty close this last year or so, but I expect you know that. Angus took Ruff home with him after the ambulance and police had been called and Charlie taken into the morgue. In fact, I think he kept Ruff with him, right up until the day of the funeral. Until you came home."

"I thought Charlie was on his own when he died. Knowing that Ruff was with him, maybe it wasn't such a lonely way to go." Rose gave Jill a quick hug as the men joined them.

"Ok. We've got them into two mobs now. Rose and Angus, we'll let yours out and help you start them on their way home.

Once you turn toward the old railway easement alongside your place, we'll get ours moving in the other direction." There were nods of agreement as the boys headed to the yards to release the smaller mob. Rose walked over to Calico, tightened the girth, untied her and mounted.

About to turn toward the cattle, just starting to move quickly out of the open gate, Greg appeared beside her, causing her to flinch in surprise as Calico threw her head back, almost yanking the reins from Rose's grip. Ruff growled.

"Rose, I can come along on the quad, give you a hand, then head back to help Dad and Jamie."

Rose smiled at him, holding the reins more firmly in hands. "Thanks Greg, appreciate it. But I have Ruff and Angus, and my herd is much smaller. You will be needed here. We'll be fine."

Greg grinned. "Of course. You have Ruff the Superdog on your team." He bent to pat Ruff, who growled again. Greg pulled his hand back quickly, a look of annoyance on his face. Rose hesitated, then said firmly, "Heel Ruff. Good boy." The dog obediently moved to the side of the horse, seemingly awaiting further instruction. Shrugging her shoulders lightly, Rose nodded at Greg and touched her heels to Calico, moving toward the herd, already starting to spread out.

"Get around Ruff," she called. The dog shot off, trotting back and forward around the back and sides of the herd, keeping them together. Waving to the others, Rose moved off, following the cattle, letting Ruff keep them bunched. Angus drove out on to the road and moved slowly alongside the railway easement, preventing any from making a dash up on to the main road.

Getting back to the break in the fence was uneventful, and Rose felt happier than she had been since the news of Charlie's death. She felt at home in the saddle, on this mare she knew so well. Ruff, although old, seemed to have a genuine spring in his step, his tongue lolling out as he moved back and forth behind the animals, he looked almost like he was smiling. Rose wondered if he would be sore tomorrow. She knew she would.

Angus parked his ute to one side near the fence and got out to help guide the animals through the fence. The young Campbell girl; Frederica although everyone called her Freddie, waved her hat, chasing one animal through the fence that threatened to turn back. She said a shy "Hello" to Rose, patted Ruff, then walked across to Angus.

"I will fix this temporarily Rose, then run Freddie back to the others. I can meet you back at the stables." Angus spoke loudly above the noise of the animals, jostling each other as they moved back into their paddock. "Can you push this lot through to the lane past the creek, then turn them into the paddock nearest the homestead? I've thrown some hay out in there, that should keep them happy. I'll come back and repair the fence properly later today."

It was on the tip of her tongue to argue with him, not liking the way he had already decided where the cattle should go. She pulled herself together. His decisions were sensible and the best for the cattle. She nodded curtly to him, seeing the smile freeze on his face as she did and taking a small amount of perverse pleasure from it.

15

Wondering how he was going to introduce a semblance of civility to his complicated relationship with Rose, Angus drove Freddie back to the temporary yards at Woolshed Lane, most of which were now packed up on the back of Neale Campbell's truck. Usually shy, the fifteen year old had become animated while chatting to Angus about his work as a vet. A real country kid, Angus could see her genuine love for the farm and animals, but with several older brothers, two already finished school and working the farm with their parents, Angus was aware there may be no room on the farm for her when she finished school.

Pulling to a stop, Freddie was opening the door when Angus said "Would you be interested in working for me at the small animal clinic over the school holidays Freddie?

Her face glowed. "You betcha, Angus. I mean, Doctor Hamilton. But isn't Melanie Mitchell your vet nurse already?"

"Angus is fine. Melanie has two weeks off during school

holidays, as her daughter, Tiffany started school this year. I open the clinic three mornings a week, but need someone there on the other days to feed and monitor any animals we have kept for ongoing treatment. There are always a few to be looked after, especially while I am out making farm calls." Angus was pleased to see Freddie's enthusiasm. She was a bright girl, may even be interested in Vet Science herself.

"Let's speak to your Dad, shall we?" Freddie flew across to her father, her curly mop of long red hair escaping from a low plait, Angus walking behind. Neale Campbell was almost knocked backwards by his daughter's enthusiastic hug and somewhat surprised by her rapid fire question.

"Angus needs help at the clinic in the school holidays, is it OK if I do it Dad? Please? I'll get all my chores done at home first, I promise!"

Neale hugged his daughter. Looking over her head he said to Angus, "if you're sure she won't be in the way, mate?"

Angus grinned at him. "She knows her way around animals, she will be a big help. Melanie is taking two weeks off and I would advertise, but this works out well."

Turning to Freddie, he said seriously, "This is paid work Freddie, not work experience. It's a real job. Full time for two weeks. If we have days with no animals overnight at the clinic, you can come on the big animal rounds with me. I have a feeling you will be a great vet nurse."

Watching Freddie dash off to her older brother, Callum, chatting in his ear as she got on the back of his motorbike, Angus knew he had made a good decision despite the spontaneity of it. He wished someone had given him such an opportunity at that age.

By the time he got back to Charlie's, Rose had locked the

cattle in to their paddock, unsaddled the mare, fed her and turned her out with the other horses. She was nowhere about, Angus assumed she had gone back to the homestead for a meal and a well-deserved rest. He checked on Topper, who was looking brighter, and noted that Rose had given the old horse fresh water and feed. With nothing left to do he drove slowly out, heading back to repair the fence properly.

He knew that Tait's were still blaming kids for letting the cattle out, but Angus had a feeling there was more to it. He couldn't put his finger on who, and why. Not yet anyway. He wondered if he should speak to the police, but had no real facts to give them. Shaking his head, he wondered, not for the first time, what it was that had sent Charlie outside before sunrise on the day he died. What caused his stroke? Angus smiled grimly. If he ever found out that someone had been there that morning ....

16

R uff growled from the veranda outside her bedroom door. Rose was disoriented for a moment, she had been dreaming of horses and cattle, and a man .... Angus? She sat up and reached for her phone. One o'clock.

The growling continued. Not like Ruff, he was generally not bothered by nocturnal goings on, possums and owls, these days. He barked, twice, then yelped. Once.

Rose was fully awake now. She pulled on jeans and t-shirt in the dark. There was something ... or someone ... outside. Not wanting to let them know she was awake, she mentally ran through the closing and locking of all external doors before she went to bed. Confident the house was secure, she called softly to Ruff. No response. No scratching at her door to the veranda. Concerned, Rose moved the curtains slightly and peered into the gloom. She could make out the shapes of trees and hedge in the rear yard, the quarter moon and starlit sky offering dim lighting. There was a dark shape laying on the lawn just beyond the veranda. It wasn't moving. Ruff.

Unlatching the door, Rose was about to rush outside to the old dog when she saw the large silhouette of a man standing under the ornamental pear tree near the hedge and back garden gate. She froze, then re-latched the door. She couldn't see his face, but he was a big man.

Heart beating quickly, Rose reached back for her phone and called the local police station. Speaking quietly, she told the on-call desk Sergeant that she had an intruder at Barrington, the homestead just a few kilometres from town.

Asked to wait, Rose moved quietly back to the veranda door, peering through the glass, the man was no longer under the tree, but Ruff hadn't moved. The desk Sergeant advised there was a police car on its way and to remain inside the house. Rose gritted her teeth, watching the shape that she believed was her grandfather's old dog, on the ground. Was he dead? She saw the tiniest of movement that may have been just a trick of the light.

She dialled the mobile number Angus had given her, days before. He answered on the second ring. "Angus, it's Rose," she spoke quietly, not sure if the intruder was still outside the house.

"Rose. What is it? Is it Topper?" he was instantly awake and pulling on his jeans as he spoke, his mobile on loud speaker.

"It's Ruff. There was someone outside. I think he's hurt. He's barely moving. Please come. Can you please come now?" Rose whispered.

"Hell. Rose. Call the police. I'm on my way. Stay inside. Go to the safest room with the best locks. Charlie's study. Go to Charlie's study." Speaking quickly, Angus grabbed his bag and was running to his vehicle.

"The police are on their way. I need to get Ruff." Rose hung up and picked up the poker from her fireplace, then unlatched the veranda door.

Stepping out, she heard police sirens heading up the driveway. Something landed at her feet and she jumped back, slamming the door. Heavy footsteps ran along the veranda, then disappeared.

Rose ran to the front door, turning on the lights as a police car pulled up in the driveway. Two officers got out, one headed around the back with a torch while the other hurried toward her. She opened the door fully, breathing fast.

"He was just here, outside my bedroom. I think he hurt my dog. I didn't get a good look at him, but he was a big man."

Sergeant Carroll drew her back into the house. "Stay inside. We will check this out."

Standing uncertainly in the entrance hall, Rose saw Angus pull up behind the police car. She ran to him, tugging on his hand.

"Around the back, Ruff is around the back on the lawn. Quickly."

Angus paused for a moment, then said "Take me through the house. The police are searching for footprints and evidence. It's best I don't add mine to the mix."

Pivoting, Rose half ran back to her room, Angus right behind her. She threw open the door from her bedroom to the veranda outside, turning on the lights as she did. Gasping, she saw Ruff still lying on the lawn, and her old Akubra hat at her feet, where it had been thrown by her unwanted visitor as the police had arrived. She hadn't seen it since the day after the funeral, the day she had ridden Topper.

Angus looked grim as he stepped out and on to the lawn,

kneeling beside Ruff. Sergeant Carroll had his torch on the old dog and Rose could see blood on one side of Ruff's head. She was beside Ruff in three steps. She sobbed once and knelt down, speaking quietly to the dog who seemed to twitch when he heard her voice.

The four of them had gathered at the kitchen table – Rose along with Angus, Sergeant Carroll and Constable Stevens. There was no sign of Ruff's attacker. Rose had made a statement, struggling to describe all she had seen in the dim light. Ruff was on blankets on the kitchen floor, breathing shallowly. He had been hit over the head by something heavy. Angus said it was touch and go. He would take the dog back to the surgery to monitor, but warned Rose he may not make it.

"And the fences were cut again, you say?" the Sergeant asked, frowning. "Charlie had complained of this over the last few months, but we had no sign it was anything other than kids. We don't know if this is related to the fence cutting Rose, but now that you have seen an adult male, we need to consider that it may be."

Angus spoke quietly, "Charlie had a theory that someone was trying to get their hands on this farm. Rosewood Beef perhaps, or others who want his access to the spring-fed creek. With the drought lasting so long, a lot would be envious of his access to water. Even so, he was careful not to pump too much from the creek, always leaving enough for others downstream." Looking at Rose, he cleared his throat. "He was worried that whoever it is would target Rose. Especially as she may not choose to return here permanently."

"We need to take this seriously. Rose, with your dog injured, I am afraid you can't stay here tonight by yourself. I can leave

Constable Stevens here until morning ..." Sergeant Carroll stopped as Rose spoke quickly.

"There's no need. I will lock up and follow Angus to the vet clinic. I want to be with Ruff." She spoke firmly, but there was a catch in her voice when she said Ruff's name.

Angus looked at the old dog, barely breathing. He didn't think the dog would make it until morning and didn't want Rose to witness his death.

"Perhaps you should go to the Taits? They are right next door," he said, ignoring the swift look of hurt that crossed her face.

With her chin up, tears glittering in her eyes, Rose said," I will go to Debbie's. I will be at the clinic in two hours to check on my dog."

Angus took Ruff gently in his arms and placed him on the front seat of his ute. He nodded to the police and drove out. Rose threw her toothbrush and a fresh shirt into a bag and locked up the homestead while the police waited. They followed her back to town.

Rose parked for an hour in the lane behind Debbie's shop and tried to get some rest. She played the incident over and over in her mind. Ruff growling. Then barking. The yelp. Nothing. The shadowy man under the tree. The hat thrown at her feet and heavy footsteps running along the timber boards as the police arrived. Angus refusing to let her come to the clinic.

Who would benefit from scaring her into leaving Barrington, heading back to Sydney? Was that what it was about? Or was it random, someone hearing that Charlie had died and wanting to break in, not realizing she was there? Ruff, bless him, warning her. He had already had such a big day mustering. He was too old; she shouldn't have taken him. Yet he had seemed so happy to be working the cattle, riding on the horse with her too. Rose cried for a moment, then blew her nose and ran her fingers through her hair. She was exhausted herself, and sore. She realised that it would be almost impossible for her to keep the farm and run it herself. She would need help. Greg Tait's face came to her for a moment, the concern he had shown earlier in the day had demonstrated a serious side. Perhaps he was more kind-hearted than she realised.

No. She shook her head. Greg had been a bully at school and a smart ass around girls. Always full of himself, he used his good looks to manipulate women. Even his mother, as smart as she is, falls for it. No Rose, she told herself, if you want to keep the farm you have to be prepared to do it alone. Yet with Angus using the land to run his stock, there was no way the farm could pay for itself. She needed to run her own stock on the land to make it profitable.

Pre-dawn light crept across town, drifting into the lane where she sat in her car. Rose breathed in deeply and drove the few blocks to the Vet Clinic. The light was on. She knew Angus would sit with Ruff. She didn't understand why he hadn't wanted her help. Had she already asked too much of him, with Topper, and now Ruff?

Angus saw the lights of the vehicle pull up. He clenched his jaw, knowing it was Rose. Sighing, he opened the door to the clinic and gestured her in. She had expected to find Ruff on the stainless steel treatment table, hooked up to a drip. Instead, he was lying on a bed of rugs on the floor, a bandage around his head, unmoving.

Glancing at Angus, Rose sat on the floor beside Ruff and put her hand on his chest. He was breathing. Just. She looked at Angus again. He knelt beside her and put his hand over hers, on the dog's chest. Looking into her eyes, he said quietly, "There is nothing more I can do, Rose. The blow to his head was hard. It has blinded him on one side, and his heart is failing. I honestly thought he would be gone by now. I wanted to save you this. His dying. That's why I didn't want you here. I'm sorry. I should have let you come."

Seeing the purple patches under her eyes, he added, "You didn't go to Debbie's did you?"

Rose shook her head. She bent over Ruff, tears falling on his head as she stroked the un-damaged area. She lifted his head gently and placed it in her lap, her back against the clinic wall.

Angus rose. Walking to the next room he put the jug on to boil and began making a pot of tea. He came out a few minutes later, steaming mugs of tea in hand. He handed one to Rose and slid down the wall beside her. Neither spoke as they sipped their tea.

Close to six, Rose had dozed off, her head resting lightly on Angus's shoulder. He didn't want to wake her, but he had to get ready for small animal clinic by 8am. He ran his hand over his stubble. He needed a shave and a shower first. Moving quietly, he left Rose and headed through to the apartment beyond the clinic.

Thirty minutes later he found Rose awake, exactly where he had left her. She had been crying. He put his hand on Ruff's chest. The loyal old dog had taken his last breath. Angus looked sadly at Rose.

"I am sorry. He was a wonderful dog. The last one Charlie trained." He gently moved Ruff's head from her lap and covered him with a clean sheet. Reaching down, his hand was warm as he helped Rose to her feet.

"I can take care of him from here Rose, you need to get

some rest. Come through to my apartment, sleep for a bit. When I am done with the small animal clinic, we can go out to Barrington and bury him."

Too tired to resist, with a long look at Ruff, Rose let Angus lead her into the apartment attached to the clinic. More like a motel room, really; kitchenette, one room with a bed and a small couch, TV and an ensuite bathroom.

"Help yourself to anything you need Rose. Try to rest." Angus spoke gently, but firmly.

Laying down on the bed, fully dressed, Rose kicked her sneakers off. Within moments of Angus closing the door, she was asleep. Dreaming of Ruff as a puppy, watching Charlie train him with stock. She hadn't been allowed to feed or play with him for the first six months. Charlie said he needed a one-man dog, and if she fussed it would ruin him. She had obeyed and when Ruff was old enough she was allowed to take him to muster. He worked for her almost as well as Charlie, but she knew his first loyalty was to her grandfather. She had often wondered what it would be like to have a cattle dog of her own, to train, to receive the unswerving love and loyalty only a dog can provide.

17

It was almost noon when Angus closed the door of the clinic. Melanie Mitchell commented more than once on the Jeep parked outside. Not in the mood for questions, Angus was more taciturn than usual with her, although gentle with the animals and their owners. Melanie had worked for the practice when Petersen ran it, and although she was good with the animals, she was inclined to gossip about their owners. For about the hundredth time, Angus thought about replacing her, but she was a single Mum with a young daughter. Melanie had thrown herself at him when he first came to town as a locum. Attractive, but not at all his type. The longer she stayed with him the pushier she became. He would need to speak to Melanie, re-establish the boundaries. Not today however. He had enough to deal with today. It would be a relief to have young Freddie Campbell here for two weeks.

He yawned. He could do with some sleep, but he needed to get Rose and Ruff home. He wondered if Rose should not stay at the homestead alone until more was known about the intruder. The killer of damn good dogs. Angus swore under his breath.

Melanie hovered after the last client left, insisting she needed to reconcile something on the computer. Angus took her by the arm, nodded at her handbag on the floor. "Head off Melanie, I will see you tomorrow. Thanks for your help with Mrs Tubb – she is definitely over-feeding her little Jack Russell. You handled her very well, the meal plan was a brilliant idea."

Smiling, Melanie shut down the computer and picked up her handbag, "Are you sure you can't come to lunch on Sunday Angus? You must get lonely here by yourself."

Holding the door open, Angus assured her he was fine.

Finally alone in the clinic, he leaned against the door for a moment before walking towards the back, where the door to his apartment remained closed.

Not knowing whether to knock or just open the door, Angus turned the handle and walked in quietly. Rose was asleep on his bed, cheeks slightly flushed, hair tumbled about her face, covering the pillow. He looked at her in his bed. A beautiful, smart, strong woman. And sexy as hell.

He stood for a moment, then cleared his throat. Rose moved toward the sound. Her eyes opened a crack. Registering Angus standing by the side of the bed, she sat up, wide awake now.

"Sorry. Fell asleep. What time is it?" She swung her long legs over the side of the bed and took the sneakers Angus handed her. "Thank you."

"It's just after noon. Are you hungry? How about I pick up something from Debbie's and we head out to your place?"

"Of course. I'm sorry, you probably have calls to make, I appreciate you letting me stay here. If you put Ruff in the back of my car, I can head back to Barrington. I have a spot in mind to bury him."

"It's no problem Rose. Ruff is already in my ute. I have calls to make past your place, later today. I want to check Topper too. Why don't you swing by Deb's and meet me out there?" Angus raised his eyebrows a little as he spoke.

Rose was about to argue, but remembering her fear from the night before, agreed.

She must be scared, Angus thought, I expected more of an argument. Angus also wanted to assure himself that the intruder was no longer at the homestead before Rose arrived.

18

Angus had laid Ruff's body, wrapped in a sheet, on the veranda and was walking back from Charlie's garden shed with a shovel as Rose drove in.

"Show me where you want him Rose, I can do this while you set out some lunch for us. I will call you when it's time." Angus spoke quietly, kindly.

Hesitating only a moment, Rose took the shovel from Angus and walked to the back of the house, under the boughs of the ornamental pear tree, Angus behind her with Ruff in his arms.

"This was his favourite spot, especially on a warm day. Right here, if you don't mind."

Laying Ruff down, Angus took up the shovel. Digging in a little he told Rose the soil was soft enough and it would not take him long.

Rose set out the lunch, a still-warm lasagne, crusty rolls, butter. A water jug and glasses. She glanced outside, Angus was still digging. Rose went to her room and changed into a light dress, brushed her teeth and her hair, before tying it up in a ponytail. She knew it made her look younger, but Angus had seen her at her worst. She added a smudge of lip gloss to her lips, slipped sandals on her feet, filled a glass with water and went outside.

He had laid Ruff in the hole and Angus took the water from her thankfully. It was a warm day. Rose reached for the shovel and began closing the grave. She had no tears left, but her heart ached for the beautiful, faithful dog. He died trying to warn her. Protecting her. Putting his glass down, Angus put one hand over hers on the shovel. Stopping, she looked into his eyes, shaded by his wide-brimmed hat.

"He was an exceptional dog, and companion, and if you believe in an afterlife, he is with Charlie now." It surprised Rose to hear the emotion with which Angus spoke the words. He had loved this old dog too. And Charlie. Angus had genuine affection for her grandfather. She would ask him about it.

They chatted comfortably over lunch. Angus reflected on days spent with Charlie, and Ruff. Rose began to see him more clearly. His honesty helped her open up too. They decided they had not the time, in that moment, to talk through the will and the consequences of Charlie's decision for both of them. But they agreed they could talk about it. And should, in the coming days.

Checking the horses before Angus left, they were pleased to see Topper had improved. He was eating and moving around with no outward sign of pain. They let him out with the other horses and Rose promised to call Angus if she had concerns when she fed them later that afternoon.

They were easy in each other's company and Rose walked

back to the homestead believing they may be able to work through the complications of the will together.

Angus offered to come out after work and stay the night, in case the intruder came back, although the police believed now it was an opportunistic intended robbery, and not specifically targeted at Rose. The re-appearance of her Akubra hat gave Rose doubts, however.

Rose explained that Debbie was staying over, they had a girl's night planned. Angus nodded and left, certain there would be no further trouble tonight with both women in the house.

ROSE BUSIED herself tidying the house for Debbie's visit. She had planned a simple menu of home-made pizza, chocolate and wine. She wondered if this was immature, then chuckled. No woman was ever too old for wine, pizza and chocolate with pals!

Being in the homestead stirred memories of growing up here. Was it unusual that she and her parents had shared this home with her grandparents? Her father had been their only child and was living here when he met her mother, a young teacher from Sydney on her first posting. Although the homestead was large, Rose wondered why her parents hadn't moved in to a home of their own.

The homestead had an airy entrance and a long hallway to the back veranda. On one side, near the front, was her grandfather's study with a two-way fireplace to her grandparents' bedroom, sitting room and a bathroom that had been added later under the veranda roofline. Beyond that, on the same side of the hall was her own spacious room. Rose still used this room, but wondered if she should move to the master bedroom.

On the other side of the hall was a formal dining room and living area, with a large fireplace between them and beautiful pressed metal ceilings, then an enormous kitchen that had been remodelled more than once over the years, and was now a large country style eat-in kitchen. It was at the kitchen table that Rose had done her homework, shared hot chocolate and cookies with Debbie, eaten her evening meals with her grand-parents.

Beyond that was the back veranda and a covered walkway to an adjoining building that would have housed the cook and maids in the early years, but had been turned into a self-contained wing for her parents when they married, with a large bedroom, study, living area, a bathroom and a small kitch-enette. Rose frowned for a moment. She remembered taking most of her meals in the main house with her grandparents, and although her parents joined them in the evenings quite of-ten, they usually made breakfast in their own section of the house and Rose could not remember spending much time with them there.

She had loved her parents but thinking back; it was her grandparents who spent time with her, taught her to ride and drive and her grandmother had shared her passion for gardening and had taught her the basics of cooking. How strange she should think of that now, years after her parents' deaths. She had spent a lot of time with her mother in her last months on earth, but still recalled how her eyes would light up when her father entered the room, and Rose would leave them. They had taken long holidays together when she was young, leaving her on the farm with her grandparents, which had not seemed odd to her. Her friendship with Debbie, and the Tait boys next door, had kept her busy and social throughout her school years.

Rose stopped at the door outside her parents' rooms, realising she had not been in this part of the house in years. She pushed the door open. It was neat and tidy; the bed was bare and there was no sign of her parents having been there at all. Her grandmother must have sorted their things years ago. Rose turned around in the main room, taking it all in. Rose wondered where their personal items were kept. There was a big trunk in her grandparents' room and another in her grandfather's study. She should look there.

In the meantime, if she had to share the house with Angus Hamilton for the next three years, perhaps he could move in here, where her parents had lived. It was self-contained and frankly, Rose felt no strong attachment to the space.

"It's so nice to have someone else do the cooking," Debbie sighed as she pushed her plate away with one hand, while reaching for the last piece of pizza with the other. Red wine in front of her and a box of chocolates beside her, she let out a little burp, then giggled.

"It was just pizza Deb, nothing fancy or gourmet like you whip up at the café," Rose mumbled around the chocolate in her mouth, while she emptied the last of the red wine into her glass.

"So glad I am taking the day off tomorrow to prepare for the engagement party, I may have a hangover in the morning. Any more wine Rose?"

"Hmm, how about Baileys now? It will be better with the chocolates," Rose got up somewhat unsteadily, taking the second empty wine bottle to the sink. She returned with shot glasses and a large bottle of Baileys.

"Might as well, I'm having too much fun to stop now." Debbie threw back the Baileys shot and pushed her empty glass back to Rose for a refill.

"Ok. So before I get to the point of no return, let me run over my duties as your Maid of Honour, for the engagement party," Rose paused, then made a wide 'oh' with her mouth. She added in a stage whisper "Do you realise I am not really a maid?" Rose snorted into her glass.

Debbie looked at her seriously. "Well, now that you mention it, I don't know how much honour you have either. I assume you are still a virgin, as all unmarried ladies should be...but if not, I may have to re-think the whole wedding party thing." Debbie waggled her eyebrows at Rose. "I, of course, will wear white on the wedding day ... or perhaps off-white. Maybe ivory. Fuck it, I'll just slip into a little black cocktail dress and be done with it! And you, my friend, can wear red!" They burst into laughter, tears rolling down their faces.

"Okay, okay," Debbie giggled "you don't have to do much. The wedding party is just you, and Greg, as Jamie's best man. It's in the woolshed. Jamie has the bar and barbecue under control. His Mum has organised salads and desserts. Honestly, we don't want a lot of speeches, just an announcement of the wedding party and the date for the wedding. It would be good if you could keep an eye on Greg, don't let him get too smashed before the speeches.

"Speaking of Greg, you know he has told Jamie that you are the girl for him and he intends to 'court' you," Debbie smiled, "perhaps we should plan a double-wedding?"

Rose took Debbie's glass and the bottle out of reach. "Do not tease me, he is already a handful. You know I have never had feelings for Greg. Definitely not my type. Far too full of himself. Please don't encourage him, I will come home far less if you do. You know you got the pick of the litter with those Tait boys." She gave Debbie what she thought was a steely look, but Debbie smiled innocently before lunging for the glass and bottle, promptly refilling it.

Debbie sighed, over-dramatically. "I got the pick of the whole town, maybe even the State. I'm just so happy, I want you to be happy too. I want EVERYONE to be happy!

"I know you told me there is no one in your life at the moment, and frankly, those city blokes remind me of the Londoners I dated, before Jamie rushed over and snapped me up. You need a good country bloke, with smarts, Rosie.

"Hey, what about Angus Hamilton? All the single girls in town," Debbie leaned in "and some not-single ones, seem to fancy him. I don't think he has taken up with anyone though. Which is strange. Perhaps he has been waiting for you Rose?"

"You are drunk, my friend, and so am I. I've told you about Charlie's will. That complicates it for me with Angus. And yes, I appreciate his attributes but he has shown no interest. It's somewhere I should not go. I also don't know how he talked Charlie into complicating his will, what sort of influence he had over him. It just doesn't add up." Rose sighed. "Let's turn in, we will struggle in the morning as it is. Um, I've made up the guest room for you."

Debbie poked her tongue out at Rose and said "What's

wrong with your big bed, we always shared it before? We can watch a movie until we fall asleep ..."

Rose walked around to Debbie's chair and gave her a big hug while reaching for the last few chocolates. "Perfect. Like old times. I'm bringing these and NOT brushing my teeth!"

19

Heading into the café for breakfast and large coffees seemed a better idea than cooking. That's where Greg found them next morning.

"Hello ladies, I see you have your sunglasses on to cut the glare of this fine day." He slid into the seat beside Rose. She looked at him over the top of her sunglasses, then winced and pushed them higher on her nose.

"A true gentleman would not make such comments," she said haughtily, "and if you want to be in our good books you will saunter over to the counter and buy two more coffees for us. Large coffees. Black, with a shot of caramel."

"No caramel for me Rose, too much like Baileys. Just straight black for me please Greg, there's a good brother-of-my-beloved," Debbie smiled at Greg, giving him a conspiratorial wink.

"Ah, I am at your beck and call, girls, as always."

As Greg went to order, Rose and Debbie looked at each other. "What were we thinking?" Debbie moaned, "two bottles of red and almost half a bottle of Baileys ..." she shook her head, frowning.

Rose nodded, then smiled at Debbie and whispered "but it was so much fun at the time ..." They both laughed.

Greg came back, set the coffees down, then moved his chair closer to Rose. She gave him a stern look.

"Don't glare at me Rose, the party is in two days and we need to catch up for a drink and talk about our wedding party duties." He placed an arm loosely over the back of her chair, just as Angus Hamilton walked in. He paused when he saw them, then nodded as he moved past to the counter. He walked back to them while waiting for his order.

"Hi Debbie, Greg. Rose." Angus gave her a slight smile. "How is our patient doing today?"

"Hi Angus, thanks. I had a quick look before I came into town. He was with the mares and eating, so I think he is on the mend. I really appreciate your help with him."

"No problem. Anytime." Angus looked up as his name was called from the counter. "My order is ready, I had better head off now." He nodded at all of them and started to move away when Debbie called out to him. "Did you get the invite I sent you for the engagement party on Saturday night Angus? I hope to see you there!"

"I'll drop in for a while, thanks Deb. Looking forward to it." Angus called back as he strode out.

～

WITH THE HORSES well fed and the cattle content with their daily serving of hay in the house paddock, Rose turned her attention to the two large steamer trunks; one in her grandparents' room and the other in Charlie's study.

Hoarding a lifetime of memories, the trunk in Charlie's study had Rose transfixed. At the top were condolence cards sent at the time of her parents' deaths, many for her mother from children she had taught over two decades. There were times it had embarrassed Rose, when out with her Mum as a young girl, that children and adults had spoken warmly to her mother, thanking her for teaching them or their children, making a difference in their lives. At the time she had given little thought to her mother's passion for teaching and love of her job. Thinking about it now, reading many heartfelt messages, Rose felt a stirring of pride, and some regret she had never acknowledged the gift of learning her mother had given so willingly, to so many, including herself. There were cards for her father too, fewer perhaps, but no less sincere. Many were for Rose and her grandparents, united in their grief.

Beneath these lay her school photos and report cards, drawings she had done as a child, a few exercise books filled with childish imaginings, short stories and poems. Rose smiled at her early writing. She had always wanted to write, had been driven to it with a passion, not unlike her mothers' love of teaching. As she grew older Rose had forgotten her dreams of becoming an author, instead moving to study communications and enter the publishing world from a different direction. Had that been on career advice provided at school? She couldn't recall.

Further down in the trunk lay some of her baby clothes, lovingly made by her grandmother, and wrapped in tissue paper. Opening the delicate packages she found knitted jackets and booties, plus sturdy miniature overalls; items she wore as a toddler, following her grandfather around the farm.

Beneath these were more report cards, this time for her father. Rose glanced through them, noting he had excelled in maths and science and received good marks for history. She couldn't remember him doing anything other than helping her grandfather with the farm. Beneath these was a large photo album. It looked slightly familiar, Rose recalled seeing it on a bookshelf in her parents living area. She marvelled at her own teenage self-absorption and lack of curiosity, as she had never looked inside it.

Sitting on the floor, her back resting against an old wing chair, she drew the album onto her lap and opened it. Her father's youthful face, smiling, standing by a small plane in an airfield. Wearing a leather jacket and jeans, he was beaming from three photos on the next page, still at the airfield. Climbing into the plane in the first shot, then sitting in the cockpit in the next, an older man in a similar outfit at the controls beside him.

Turning another page, every photo at an airfield and with planes; in them, on them, washing them. Rose recalled his fascination with planes, particularly those flown in World War Two, and the many books on the subject littering his bookshelves. Turning more pages, more planes, but now her mother was featuring. Hair tied back and a bright scarf around her neck, laughing up into her father's face. Another of her in the cockpit with him. In the cockpit with him? Did that mean her Dad had his pilot's licence? She hadn't known. She had no idea he had this other life.

Momentarily believing it must have been when he was

young and courting her Mum, she gasped as she turned page after page. Her father in every picture, and sometimes her mother, getting older. Her mother obviously pregnant, her father boosting her up into the small plane from behind, his hands on her bottom, both laughing into the camera. Toward the end of the album there were less of her mother, but her father in each one, now with grey in his hair, another with a light beard. Rose remembered that, she had been in her teens and he had grown his beard for a month. It had been a joke with her mother that although he had dark hair, his beard would be red. He had won that bet.

Laying the album in her lap, Rose thought about her parents. Had she really known them at all? Her father had never taken her to the airfield, or up in a plane. She had not known he could fly. Why the secrecy? Had her grandparents known about his passion for flying? Why had he not made it his career? She recalled he had worked without complaint on the farm with Charlie, but she had never seen him light up when working with cattle, horses or dogs as he was in the photos of him flying.

Who could she ask now? If Charlie had not known, then no one else would. Douglas Barlow had hinted her father had stayed on the farm, the only child, out of duty to her grandfather. Had Charlie somehow stopped him from following his dreams?

～

THE LIGHTS on the woolshed could be seen from a kilometre away, as Rose drove past the Tait homestead toward the festivities. It was beautifully set up, with fairy lights and fine fabric draped under the ceiling. There were tables laden with salads and desserts down one side of the woolshed and the barbeque was just outside the main doors, manned by Jamie's father, Ross and some of his mates. Jamie had his own mates running the bar set up across the room from the food. Hay bales were set around the edges for seating, with a space in the middle for dancing. Two guitarists were perched on bar stools, with microphones, an amp and massive speakers, playing country rock music and bantering with each other between songs. They looked familiar. Rose thought they may have been a year or two below her in school. A few people were standing around on the dance floor, chatting. No one dancing yet, she noted.

Several people smiled and nodded as she walked in, dressed in bootleg jeans, boots and an emerald green silk top with shoestring straps and a low back. She had a jacket over her arm, but the night was balmy and the woolshed warm. Debbie saw her and ran over, making her multi-coloured maxi skirt swoosh across the floorboards, an off the shoulder white blouse accentuating her olive complexion and blonde hair.

The girls gave a little squeal and hugged each other. Heads turned toward them. Debbie with her dark skin and blonde hair was a little shorter than Rose, whose own long dark auburn hair and creamy complexion was a perfect foil for Debbie's colouring. Many people in the room remembered the girls in their teens and smiled to see them together again.

Debbie went to Jamie at the door, joining him to welcome more arriving guests. Rose wandered over to the salad bar, smiling and chatting with locals, many of them familiar to her.

Ross Tait used the microphone to announce, "The steak and

burgers are ready and the salads are good to go. Help yourselves and we will have the speeches in about half an hour."

Guests moved toward the food, then took up seats on the hay bales, chatting easily together.

Rose jumped when Greg came up behind her quietly and slipped his arm around her waist. She had elbowed him in the midriff before realizing what she was doing. Something had scared her and Rose realised in that moment that she had not processed her fear of the shadowy figure who killed Ruff. She had not told Debbie, not wanting anything to spoil her day, telling her only that Ruff had passed away. Only Angus knew the danger she had been in.

Greg made an 'oomph' sound and doubled over. "Bloody hell, Rose, I wouldn't hurt you," he wheezed. Jamie appeared, his father by his side.

"You know better than that Greg, don't be so familiar with Rose. You deserve whatever you get. Don't treat her like a football groupie!" Jamie was more frustrated than angry at Greg. "And don't get pissed tonight. At least not until after the speeches, or I will bloody well get another best man!"

Ross Tait put his hand on his son's shoulder. "Lovely to see you Rosie. Don't let this rough bugger mistreat you. Greg, son, come and get some food and sit with your mother and I." Ross steered Greg away as Rose mumbled something about, "sorry, you startled me."

Jamie put his arm around Rose and gave her a gentle squeeze. "Sorry Rose, I know he is my big brother, but I just don't think Greg has grown up. A bit too spoilt during his footy years I think. Let me fetch you some food, I'm getting something for Deb now. Sit with her, she is up near the band." He pointed Debbie out, chatting to her staff from the café.

Rose smiled gratefully at Jamie. He really had turned into a lovely man. Debbie and he are a good fit.

Turning to head toward Debbie, Rose almost bumped into someone. Stepping back with a quick apology, she realised it was Freddie Campbell, standing shyly before her.

"Freddie!" Rose gave her a quick hug, then stood back and said "you look very nice." Freddie blushed, making the freckles across her nose more pronounced. Long legged as a young horse, and almost as skittish, Freddie was as tall as Rose and wearing a similar outfit of dark jeans and boots. Her forest green blouse, tucked into the front of her jeans and loose at the back, was a darker shade than Rose's silk top.

"Hi Rose, you look nice too."

"You got the memo that anyone with a tinge of ginge should wear green with their jeans tonight?" Rose grinned at her young friend, putting her at ease. "We could be twins. Only a mother could tell us apart."

Freddie laughed and said "no one would mix us up. I'm red and curly. The boys tease me all the time about it!" She nodded at her older brothers, helping at the bar. All of them had bright red hair.

Leaning in, Rose whispered, "Ah, but Freddie, your brothers are all going to lose their hair by the time they're thirty, like your Dad." She nodded at Freddie's parents, standing together near the bar, Neale Campbell's hair faded and receding. "While you, young lady, will lose a bit of your curl and your hair will deepen to a rich auburn in the next few years. I know mine did."

Amazed Freddie looked at Rose closely. "Really? Your hair was red, like mine?"

"Redder. Curlier too I think." Rose enjoyed the play of emotions across her young friend's face.

"Awesome."

"I hear you are going to work at the Vet's over the school holidays. Looking forward to it?"

"It's the best thing that's ever happened to me! I will learn so much from Angus, I mean Doctor Hamilton. I can't wait!" With her face lit up, Rose glimpsed the beautiful young woman Freddie would become and admired her genuine enthusiasm.

"Would you like to do Vet Science at Uni Freddie?"

"I don't know; I've always wanted to work with animals. Horses mostly. But ours are gone, the boys prefer motorbikes and quads. Vet nurse perhaps, or farrier or horse breaker. I don't get to ride now ..."

Rose interrupted, as an idea took shape in her mind, "Freddie! I've got an idea! Are you up for more work after school and weekends?"

Confused, Freddie smiled back. "Sure. What do you need Rose?"

"Help with my horses. I have to go back to work in Sydney in another week and Angus will check on them and even feed them daily, but they aren't getting any exercise at all. Calico, the mare I rode on Monday when we mustered, needs to be ridden and another mare, Cotton, hasn't been ridden in a long time. Topper can be a bit snarly, but if you're gentle, he'll let you brush him down. There's a young filly, Storm, that's not broken in. She just needs to be handled; brushed, walked a bit. What do you say Freddie, are you interested?"

Beaming and talking at once, Freddie threw her arms around Rose, hugging her tightly. "I love your horses Rose. Charlie would let me bring them in for a feed when I went over with Dad after school sometimes. I've never ridden any of them, and I've always feared Topper, but I'd love to do it. I can get there on my bike, easy!"

Laughing, Rose linked arms with Freddie and said "Let's check with your parents then, see what we can arrange."

20

Angus hesitated a moment before he got out of his car. He liked this town, these people. He wanted to put down roots here, feel part of the community. He sighed inwardly. It wasn't always easy; he had been an outsider all his life. His father had been with the army and they moved a lot when he was young until he was killed during an incident in East Timor when Angus was fifteen.

He and his mother and younger sister Meggie had moved to his grandparents' farm near Goulburn, where Angus spent some very happy years, discovering his love of animals. His grandfather had died while Angus was studying Veterinary Science in Gatton, Queensland. Angus had assumed he would leave the farm, small as it was, to him and his sister. He left it to Angus's mother, his grandmother already showing early signs of dementia.

Angus didn't blame his mother for selling the farm. She had left it to marry his father when she was only eighteen and had no interest in the property. The proceeds of the farm bought her a small unit on the coast in northern New South Wales, where she cared for her mother, the dementia now well advanced. He admired his mother greatly, most people would have put Gran in a nursing home by this stage. But he recalled his mother promising she would always care for her parents, as they had cared for her, Angus and Meggie after his father died.

Angus only saw his Mum a few times a year. He needed to employ a locum when he had days off, and business had been tough lately, the drought taking its toll on locals. The whole town had tightened their belts, when farmers struggled to make money, the retail, commercial and professional sectors also suffered. People only bought necessities, changed their vehicles less often, put off going to the dentist and optometrist unless the need was urgent. There were quite a few empty shops in town and Angus knew that Debbie had laid one staff member off, working a little more herself. He hadn't seen Meggie since she was home more than two years ago. She had travelled to San Francisco for an au pair position several years ago and was still over there, working at a winery in the Napa Valley. He missed her and hoped she would come back for a visit soon. He hoped that he might be able to invite his Mum and sister to visit him at Barrington, if he was able to come to an arrangement with Rose. If Gran was able to travel it would be lovely to have them stay for a few days, or longer. He hoped he might have a home of his own one day. And a family.

Angus had no trouble attracting women, but he wanted one who loved the country, animals and farming, like he did. Many of the women around here were looking to get out and head to the city. Old Charlie had talked Rose up no end, but in his heart he knew she was not the one. Her love of the country was strong, but her career and life in the city were stronger drivers, he thought. Still, he was glad he had worked the deal with Charlie, as it would see him in a position to offer to buy the land in three years, when Rose was ready to sell. The drought would surely break and the town would pick up. Charlie had known it may work out this way. He was a lot like his own grandfather and Angus missed them both.

The speeches were beginning as Angus made his way into the room, smiling and nodding at those he knew before heading to the bar to grab a beer. Stubby in hand he leaned back against the side of the bar and watched while Ross and Jill Tait proudly announced the engagement and welcomed Debbie to their family. Debbie's parents were included and photos were taken and toasts made.

Jamie and Debbie took over the microphone while their parents went back to their seats, beaming proudly. Jamie held Debbie's hand and declared he had known he would marry her since he was thirteen years old. Debbie responded by telling stories of how mean Jamie had been to her during their early teens and had the room laughing along with her.

Jamie took back the microphone and said "Debbie, everyone knows that young boys don't know how to express their feelings, so pulling your pony tail, hiding your school bag and bombing you in the swimming hole were just my way of telling you I liked you," he grinned at her.

"Oh, I knew. But I had to go all the way to London for you to get your act together and come and tell me," she turned into his arms and kissed him hard on the lips. The room erupted into laughter, clapping and stomping.

The happy couple gestured for Rose and Greg to come and stand with them. Jamie took the microphone, and with his arm around Debbie and Greg on his other side, Rose stepped close to Debbie and linked their arms.

"The wedding party is before you. My big brother and best mate, Greg, is best man," Jamie grinned as he spoke. Debbie leaned into the microphone and said "and my oldest and dearest friend Rose Gordon has agreed to be my maid of honour.

"We don't want to wait too long to be married, so mark in your diaries, six months from now, we will celebrate our wedding and we invite you all to join us! Official invitations will follow."

Jamie swung Debbie around in his arms while the crowd clapped and took photos. Angus watched from the bar. The four young people at the front of the room looked happy and very comfortable together. He noticed that Greg had come around to stand beside Rose, with his arm around her waist. She did not look unhappy, from where he stood. He took another swig of his beer as the music kicked in and the four young people started the dancing. Soon the floor was crowded, the music pumping, and the lights seemed dimmer.

A lot of the older generation had cleaned up the salads, leaving desserts out for any late-takers, and headed back to the homestead to watch proceedings from afar. Angus was in conversation at the bar with Jim Fraser, one of the major Black Angus breeders in the district, discussing the recent buy ups of local land by Rosewood Beef, undercutting local producers.

Jim said that several local properties had already been sold, before they were officially on the market, some of them in financial difficulties before selling. Three years of drought had hit a lot of farmers very hard. He was curious to understand how Rosewood Beef had the local knowledge to make offers before the properties were listed. Someone local must be working with them. Angus had to agree, there had been too many sales to make it coincidental.

While listening to Jim, Angus noticed Rose had left the dance floor and was heading to the bar. He straightened up and shook Jim's hand, who turned to another farmer standing with them. Rose smiled at Angus as she came over.

"Hi. I didn't see you arrive."

"The speeches had started, so I haven't been any further than the bar." He passed her a cold beer.

"I haven't had beer in years. I'm a wine girl these days. But it is hot on that dance floor." Rose lifted the stubby and drank half of it in a few big gulps. She wiped her mouth with the back of her hand, and an exaggerated "aaah."

He chuckled. "You don't seem that out of practice."

"You can take the girl out of the country..." she winked at him.

He looked at her for a moment, admiring the colour in her cheeks brought on by dancing, her thick hair falling over her shoulders and the green silk of her blouse accentuating the rise and fall of her breasts. She noticed him looking and drew herself up a bit, saying with a cheeky grin "I am not a heifer at the market, Mr Hamilton ..."

He almost snorted beer out his nose and they collapsed into each other, laughing. Angus straightened, set his empty beer back on the bar and took hers from her hand.

"How about a dance Rose?"

"Sure thing," she answered. He led her onto the dance floor and held her hand, swinging her around to the beat of the music.

"Who taught you to dance, mister? You have some fine

moves." Rose was relaxed, feeling safe and just a little playful, in Angus's arms.

He pulled her against him for a moment. "My grandma used to get me dancing in the living room when I was about fifteen. I wouldn't admit it at the time, but it was fun."

"Oh, where are your grandparents living?"

He paused for a moment, then pulled her closer as a slow song started. "They used to live in Goulburn, had a small farm there. My grandfather died when I was at university. Mum sold the farm and bought a small place on the northern New South Wales coast, where she looks after Gran. I get up there when I can. She will come down and visit once I have a proper home for her to stay in. The rooms at the back of the vet clinic aren't suitable.

"I have a younger sister working in California. We're close, but again, I only see her every couple of years."

21

L eaning against him, Rose could feel the emotion in his voice, although he said the words lightly enough. She liked him for sharing a bit of his history. She could understand how he had become attached to Charlie.

At that moment Greg bumped into them as he was leaving the dance floor, drunk. "I believe you have my girl in your arms, Hamilton." Greg slurred.

"Stop it Greg! Go home and sleep it off," Rose spoke sharply, her body now stiff in Angus's arms.

"But Rose, it's always been you!" Greg was getting louder and Rose could see a few people turned toward them.

"Come outside Greg, we'll talk there." Rose coaxed, giving him a smile. She stepped out of Angus's arms, smiling briefly at him, then took Greg's hand and led him toward the door. Outside she let go of his hand and said firmly, "I am not your girl Greg and never will be. Don't make a scene and ruin the party. Why don't you sleep it off at the house, or in your car. You already have a black eye from the other night, which you know you deserved."

Greg straightened up, then held Rose by the hand. "Don't speak to me like a child Rose. I'm not that drunk. We would make a good team and you need someone to help you with the farm. Think about it Rose."

Pulling her hand from his, she spoke quietly, not wishing to make a scene but also unwilling to lead him on. "We can talk next week Greg but I am going back to the party now."

Greg leaned down, gave her a hard kiss on the mouth before she could move away. Rose glanced around to see if anyone had noticed. Thankfully, everyone was watching the dancing inside.

From the side of the woolshed, walking back from her car with a blanket to cover her daughter sleeping on a hay bale, was Melanie, Angus's vet nurse. "Stuck-up bitch," she whispered under her breath, "she has two of the best-looking men in the district keen on her."

Rose walked inside to find Angus leaning on the bar, two beers in hand. He handed her one, eyebrows raised.

Rose shrugged, reluctant to discuss her thoughts on Greg, then took a long drink from the stubby.

They stood watching the dancing from their spot by the bar. Jamie and Debbie were glued together, barely moving to the music, looking at each other, speaking softly.

"Nice couple," Angus nodded toward them. Rose smiled, feeling somewhat choked up at the obvious happiness of her friends.

"You won't find nicer anywhere."

Angus took her hand and tugged her toward the dance floor again. "Why don't we join them?

She looked at him for a moment, then said "hold that thought. I need to powder my nose, but I'll be right back."

Rose handed him her empty beer and walked toward the line of porta-loos. They were all occupied, so she stood at the side of the wool shed in shadows, while she collected her thoughts. She really is attracted to Angus, yet it's complicated. At least they were talking and getting to know one another.

She stepped forward as a toilet door swung open and came face to face with Melanie Mitchell. She looked somewhat wobbly in her high heels. Totally unsuited to a woolshed party, Rose thought.

Rose nodded and stepped around her and was surprised when Melanie grabbed her arm. She could smell rum on her breath as she leaned in and snarled, "so which one do you want Rose Gordon? Greg or Angus? Or are you planning to play them, have them both? Everyone is talking about you in town. Rose Gordon is back, and she is screwing Greg Tait, and Angus Hamilton ..."

Raising her eyebrows, Rose removed Melanie's hand from her arm. "My actions are none of your business Melanie Mitchell and I resent what you are implying...."

Melanie interrupted, pulling a face. "*I resent what you are implying.* You always were a stuck-up bitch! I know you spent the night with Angus the other night. Oh, I know your dog died. Wouldn't put it past you to organise that either ..."

Furious, Rose raised her hand, wanting to strike Melanie for the vicious lies, but stopped herself, taking in how drunk Melanie was. Instead, she turned away without another word.

Back in the woolshed she saw Angus start toward her from the bar. Greg Tait was standing with his father, saw Rose and also began walking toward her. Rose hesitated.

The band struck up a Tina Turner song, Nutbush and Rose laughed out loud as Debbie grabbed her hand and with Jamie and a bunch of their school friends got up to line dance. It was something they had done at parties during their school days many times.

Joining in with gusto, Rose laughed her way through the entire song, often turning at the wrong moment as she struggled to remember the moves. She noted that Melanie had returned and had dragged Angus on to the dance floor, where he was performing quite an accomplished version of the dance.

Greg had disappeared. Hopefully to sleep it off, Rose thought.

The song ended, and the band followed up with an old Kenny Rogers song. Rose went to grab a soda. Leaning back on the bar, drink in hand, she noticed that Angus was still with Melanie, doing a slow fox trot around the floor. It looked like he was holding her close, her head on his shoulder. They moved well together. Could they be an item? Is that why she was so pissed off earlier?

Rose chatted with locals at the bar, declining a couple of invitations to dance. She was sitting with Debbie when Angus appeared by her side.

He leant over to Debbie, giving her a light kiss on the cheek, saying quietly. "Congratulations Deb, great party. It's already been a big year for you, with the café and now a wedding to plan. Well done. Jamie is a lucky man."

His words were genuine, Debbie smiled up at him. "Thank you Angus." Somewhat cheekily she added, "Perhaps I should thank you for the success of the café, as you are by far my best customer." Turning to Rose she whispered loudly, "He is not an accomplished chef, is our Angus."

The three of them laughed. "You're right Deb. But why would I improve my cooking skills when I can so easily get my daily nutritional needs from Coffee is my Calling?"

Looking at Rose, Angus held out his hand, "another dance Rose?" She hesitated, looking around for Melanie. She seemed busy chatting to some other mums in the corner where a few of the younger children were curled up under blankets after exhausting themselves running around outside.

"Sure." They moved on to the dance floor, moving together easily. He was certainly a good dancer, making it very easy to follow his moves. Jamie and Debbie were beside them, wrapped in each other's arms, rocking gently from side to side.

With her boots on, they were almost cheek to cheek and Rose could feel the lean length of his body against hers. His mouth brushed her ear. Was that deliberate? She felt a languid warmth flowing through her as his hand slid down to the small of her back, pressing her gently against him.

He wouldn't hold me like this if he was having an affair with Melanie. Perhaps he is a free agent. I really should get to know him better, understand why Charlie made his will this way. Perhaps I can understand his relationship with Charlie when he speaks of how much he misses his own grandfather.

She turned her face to Angus to speak to him, at the same moment he turned to her. Their lips touched, briefly. Electricity ran through her body and she straightened. He felt it too, missed a beat of the music and stepped on her toe. They moved apart a little, looking at each other.

Angus gave a slight smile and pulled her close again, once more in time to the music. He murmured in her ear. "There is something here Rose. Between us. I would like to take some time to get to know you. In a less public place."

She nodded, unable to speak for a moment. She felt some-thing. Definitely. But what? Passion? No, it felt deeper than that. Feelings, certainly. But what?

The song changed, and they moved apart. Angus held her left hand loosely in his right. "Would you like me to escort you home Rose?" His voice was low, tinged with emotion. Rose understood his meaning and was considering it when she saw him frown, looking over at the corner where Melanie and the children were.

Melanie had a large tote over her shoulder, teetering in skinny jeans and stiletto heels, while she tried, unsuccessfully, to gather up her sleeping daughter. It looked like she was intending to leave, and it was clear she was in no condition to drive.

Angus looked around, no one else had noticed. Melanie had finally gathered her daughter in her arms and was heading uncertainly toward the door. He glanced at Rose. "Stay here. I will help her with Tiffany and see if she has someone organised to drive."

Rose moved back to sit with Debbie and Jamie, watching while Angus spoke quietly to Melanie, taking the sleeping child in his arms. He glanced briefly at Rose as he walked toward the door. Melanie followed unsteadily until another young woman, one of the mums, took the bag from her shoulder and helped her walk outside.

Debbie looked at Rose. "Angus, hey?"

Rose shrugged. "I don't know Debbie. I feel there is some-thing there. But Melanie spoke to me earlier. She was upset. Does she have a claim on Angus?"

"Melanie put it around that he is taken, and that may have stopped others from seeking his company. But I really haven't seen anything from Angus to indicate his interest. Until tonight that is. He danced with her and was pretty quick to help with her little girl. Although she is very drunk...."

"Well, let's see if he comes back in. If he takes her home ...." "Rose trailed off. Her feelings for Angus, just minutes ago, seemed to deflate.

An hour later, most of the guests had left and a core group of young ones were having a quiet drink as the band packed up their gear. Angus had not returned.

Rose had arranged for Freddie to come over after breakfast to introduce her to the horses.

Her parents had been pleased when Rose outlined her thoughts but had insisted Freddie not be paid. "She was devastated when we sold the last horses a couple of years ago, but we just didn't have the feed. Just to have her able to ride again, and such quality stock horses as yours, is enough payment. We'll drop her over after school and on weekends, subject to homework considerations, of course." The last bit was for Freddie's benefit, who was nodding enthusiastically.

Waving them off, Freddie dashing back for another hug, had given Rose a glow of warmth. She could see potential in Freddie, and quiet strength. It would be a good arrangement.

With her small handbag over her shoulder and her jacket across her arm, Rose stepped over to her friends.

"Great party guys." Rose hugged Debbie, then Jamie. "I'm off. I will chat to you tomorrow. Let me know if you want me to come over to help clean up."

"No need Rose. Mum and her cronies will have it all done before breakfast," Jamie laughed. "Rose, are you OK to drive? How much have you had to drink?"

"I'm good, thanks. A couple of beers early on, a champagne

with the speeches, then just soda water from there." Jamie nodded, satisfied she was OK to drive herself home.

Rose pulled her jacket around her shoulders as she walked out to her car. It was well after midnight. There were a few vehicles left in the paddock beside the woolshed, one of them was the ute she knew belonged to Angus. She stopped for a moment. So he had driven Melanie home in her car. Nice gesture from a boss.

Tired and suddenly unaccountably flat, Rose sighed to herself as she eased her car out on to the driveway. Just when she was getting to know Angus and gain some understanding of the man her grandfather had liked so much and who would, if she followed Charlie's will, be living in her home for the next three years.

22

C hecking the house was securely locked, Rose went to bed. She lay in bed thinking about the night, the homestead, the farm. She thought about buying a puppy, a working dog, to train. If she could get back every other weekend, she could do it. Possibly finish breaking the filly in too. Rose sighed. Pipe dreams. She would have to be here full time to train a young dog. But maybe she could work the filly. Freddie helping with the horses regularly would make the filly quieter, more used to being handled.

Rose woke, disappointed she had not had the chance to continue her 'conversation' with Angus. It felt like an opportunity lost. It had slipped between her fingers like quicksilver.

Coffee in hand, Rose strolled outside, around to Ruff's grave, thinking to stand in the shade for a few minutes. Stopping short as she approached the spot where Ruff lay at rest, she saw large footprints all over the fresh mound of earth. Rose hesitated, glancing around quickly. There was no one nearby, and she had not heard a vehicle during the night or early morning. Shivering for a moment, she wondered if she should notify the police.

There was someone sneaking around at night. She needed to be vigilant. Perhaps she should get another dog. Remembering Ruff as a puppy and young dog brought tears to her eyes. She could recall her grandfather training Ruff when the dog was young. She missed them both.

The sound of a vehicle moving slowly up the driveway interrupted her thoughts. Walking around to the front of the homestead, coffee cup still in hand, she saw Neale Campbell in his old Landrover, Freddie perched up beside him.

Freddie was out almost before her father had come to a complete stop. Dressed appropriately in jeans and riding boots, a wide brim hat in her hands, Freddie said hello to Rose and bounced from one foot to the other while her father got out and strolled over.

"Morning Rose. How did you end up after the party?"

"Morning Neale. Good thanks, I left not long after you. Once the band stopped most folk started to drift off." Rose smiled warmly at her neighbour, noting the twinkle in his eye as he prolonged Freddie's anticipation.

"I can come back over in a couple of hours, pick her up. You'll be tired of her by then." Neale pulled a pipe and tobacco pouch from his pocket and proceeded to slowly fill, then light it.

"Daaad!"

Smiling, Rose felt a measure of sympathy for her young friend. Charlie used to treat her in a very similar way, when she was younger. She could recall the frustrated excitement of having to wait for something special.

"I think we'll do well together. Today is an introduction to the horses. I'd like to take a ride with Freddie, see how she handles the mares, then we will work out what she can do by herself, and what should wait until I am here, or Angus." Rose could see Freddie nodding, a pleading look at her father.

"All right then, love. Do as Rose says, now." Neale gave his daughter a playful nudge, grinned at Rose, then returned to his vehicle, driving out slowly.

"Come into the house a moment Freddie. I just need my boots and a hat and we'll be right to go."

Hesitating on the top step, Freddie's face dropped. "I'm sorry about Ruff. He was an amazing dog."

"Me too," was all Rose could say.

Laying some hay in the yards, Rose called the horses, who arrived within moments, it seemed. Rose walked among them with Freddie, who spoke quietly to them. She already knew their names and despite admitting she was scared of him, bravely patted Topper on his neck.

In the tack room they gathered up Rose's saddle and bridle for Calico and a saddle and bridle for Cotton. Working together, they saddled the horses. Rose could see how competent Freddie was, and her quiet confidence seemed to soothe the horses.

Initially thinking she would ride Cotton, knowing she hadn't been ridden in a long time, and put Freddie on Calico, she noted a lovely bond between the two from the start and changed her mind. They'd put the other horses back out to the paddock and mount in the yard, so Cotton would be contained if she played up.

Standing side by side, reins in hand, Rose grinned at Freddie. "Ready?"

Grinning back, Freddie responded with a nod and "Yup."

Left foot in stirrup, a bounce on tiptoe then the right flung over their horses, both women settled their bums into their saddles at the same time. The mares, Calico and Cotton, didn't move a muscle.

"Walk her around the yard, see if the stirrups are the right length."

Freddie did as she was asked and Cotton responded beautifully. Rose noted how well Freddie sat the horse, her hands light on the reins. She was a natural.

Opening the gate from her saddle, Rose led the way out to the lane that led toward the creek. Taking the mares through their paces, chatting easily as they rode, they found themselves at the paddocks near the state forest fence line. Rose checked on the mend in the fence, noting how well Angus had repaired it. She should thank him for that. Heading back they cantered slowly up the lane. The Australian stock horse is bred to cover long distances in a slow energy-conserving canter, less jarring for the rider than a trot.

Exhilarated, they had just reached the yard when Neale Campbell pulled up in his Landrover. Rose gave the reins of both mares to Freddie to take through to the yard, tie up and unsaddle.

"She's a natural Neale. I'd trust her with any of my horses." Standing together outside the yard, each with a boot on the bottom rail, Rose and Neale spoke quietly, watching Freddie unsaddle and brush both mares, before giving them a small feed of oats and a drink.

"She is Rose. This is a special gift you've given her. Frankly, we couldn't afford to keep the horses, with only Freddie still riding and the drought going on like it has. We planned to keep one for her, but don't have the setup you have here, with stables and tack room and a proper horse yard. The boys had no interest and I guess we thought Freddie would leave to go to Uni in a couple of years ... she really didn't complain much either."

Touching him lightly on his sleeve, Rose said, "Freddie is a smart girl and emotionally mature. She understood your reasons. The family, and the farm, comes first. She told me today while we rode. She has no resentment about it. That's what makes her so special."

Neale looked at his daughter for a moment, happily patting Cotton while she ate her oats. Turning to Rose, he had moisture in his eyes. "We are lucky, Rose. A houseful of boys, my big sons, then this wonderful creature when we had given up hope of ever having a girl. The boys will stay, farmers all of them, but she will leave us one day." Shaking his head, as if to erase the image, he watched as his daughter let the horses back into the paddock where they kicked up their heels and galloped toward the gum trees.

"Hmm. She may not leave for good Neale. It's in her blood to stay here. She's a country girl, and a Campbell. I have a feeling she won't stray far, or long."

"Thank you, Rose."

❧

WITH THE CAMPBELLS' gone, Rose went through her grandfather's books again in his study, hoping to find an explanation for his decision to leave the stock to Angus.

Her grandfather didn't have his accounts on computer, although Rose knew he used a local accounting firm to complete his tax obligations. She unlocked the three drawer filing cabinet, finding the usual stud files and farming collateral in the top two drawers. The bottom drawer yielded results. There she found a stack of handwritten ledgers, going back dozens of years.

Rose pulled out three or four from the top of the pile. Opening up the most recent one, she saw her grandfather's messy scrawl, almost indecipherable, on each side of the ledger. She frowned, trying to read the entries. Perhaps she should just get a copy of the electronic accounts from the tax agent in town?

Pushing the first one aside, she randomly drew another from the pile. Three years ago and all the entries were in the small, perfectly formed letters from the hand of her grandmother. Much easier to understand, Rose read through the income and outgoings over several months.

Frowning, she noted that there was a large monthly payment marked 'mortgage'. Rose sat back. Surely not. Her grandfather had always told how his own grandparents had paid for the land and built the house with cash from their cattle and grain sales. Why would they take a mortgage so late in their lives?

Rose flipped open another ledger; this one from eight years earlier. She smiled when she saw the neat hand of her father. He always printed in capital letters, believing his left-handed writing was too difficult to read. There was no mortgage at that time, so her grandparents must have taken it out more recently. She noticed that her father took much larger wages than her grandparents did, at the time. She nibbled at her bottom lip. Her parents had enjoyed many weekends away and holidays when her mother wasn't teaching. Was this for her father's flying passion? Did her father's secret hobby stretch their budget? Did they live beyond their means? But her mother worked, so they would have had her teaching income too.

Her grandparents had rarely left the district – only to go to the royal show in Sydney and they had been to the UK once when she was young, to meet relatives her grandmother had always written to but never met.

Sitting back, Rose thought about her own life. She had never questioned that she had no university debt to pay, it had been covered by the 'farm' her father, and then grandparents, had assured her. She had worked part-time while studying, using her own money for rent, car payments and her planned trip to London. She remembered times during school years and uni when the region had been in drought and recalled her grandfather selling a lot of stock after her father died. Had he left a debt that her grandparents had to cover? His plane perhaps?

Could it be the mortgage was taken out to help her through uni? She wished she had thought to ask more about her inheritance. She hadn't questioned the lump sum that came to her from her father's will, which she had used to buy her two-bedroom flat in Kirribilli, outright.

On a mission now, Rose sorted through the ledgers until she found the one that covered the year her mother died, with her father passing shortly after. Taking a deep breath, she opened the ledger. It was in her father's writing, at first, then her grandmother took over halfway through. Rose noted that her father had claimed a wage for himself and her mother. She had been too sick to teach, but why would she have needed a wage? She had died only six months after her diagnosis and Rose felt sure health insurance covered the medical bills. Yet the wages had increased each month.

Turning to the months after her father's passing, where her grandmother's hand recorded expenses and income, she saw the mortgage entry for the first time. The amount was staggering; more than her little apartment had cost. The two months before recorded an increase in income from the sale of stock. It seemed her grandparents had tried to cover a debt through selling stock, but still needed the loan.

Turning back to the most recent ledger, in her grandfather's handwriting, she noted the mortgage payment was no longer recorded. She reached for the ledger of the previous year. Reading through each month she finally found the entry that made sense of her current situation. The sale of the stock to 'A. Hamilton' came first, in the income column, then recorded neatly the day after in the expenses column, the mortgage was marked 'paid in full'.

The amounts were identical.

Slamming the ledger closed, Rose pushed back the chair and strode into her room. Opening her closet, she rummaged around until she pulled out a blue-spotted bikini. Undressing quickly, she pulled the bikini on, tying the narrow strings of the top behind her neck. She glanced quickly in the mirror as she pulled her hair back into a tight plait. She hadn't worn this bikini since her late teens, and her bust was fuller these days, although her hips were still narrow and her tummy flat.

Don't care, she thought. *I have nicer swimsuits in Sydney, but didn't think to bring one home. It's not something you pack for a funeral.*

Jumping into her Jeep, Rose drove through the farm to the creek. She laid a towel on the grassy bank, before splashing into the shallows, then diving under when she reached the deeper swimming hole. She felt unaccountably angry. She wasn't sure if it was at herself, or her father. That her grandparents, who had been caring and consistent her whole life should have needed to take a mortgage, saddened her. Was it just to pay her inheritance? Was there more to it? If she had known, would she have refused the money and not bought the beautiful little apartment by the water in Sydney? Why didn't she ever question this? How selfish she was!

The cold water helped expunge the myriad of thoughts going around in her head, and after a few minutes she relaxed and floated languidly in the water. Maybe Angus Hamilton was the good guy. She should think more on that. He was coming to dinner this very evening, she would show him the ledgers and perhaps he will be able to answer some of her questions.

About to get out, Rose heard a motorbike on the other side of the creek. The state forest side. She scrambled out, hearing the motorbike come closer, and quickly towelled herself off and pulled on her tee shirt. Her heart was racing. Was it kids that were letting the cattle out? Or someone more sinister? The person who killed Ruff? What else is he capable of?

"Hey! Rose! It's me, Greg." Relieved, Rose saw Greg make his way to the bank of the creek. He was in shorts, no shirt. He stepped into the creek, then dived under, surfacing close to where she stood on her side of the creek. Rose laid her towel down on the grassy edge and relaxed on to it, raking her fingers through her wet, tangled hair.

Greg swam a few strokes to the other side, then back again, before stepping out, throwing himself on the ground beside her.

"Sorry if I startled you. It's quicker to get to the swimming hole through the state forest these days. Dad and Jamie have taken a few of the gates out of the boundary fence because of the cattle rustling."

Rose looked at Greg. He was sober, relaxed, and speaking seriously for a change. She liked him like this. He was also a very well built man. Large and muscular, although lean through the hips, he still had an athlete's body. Pity he could be such a dick, though.

"How long has this been going on? The fence cutting and cattle getting out? Your folks think it's kids, but it seems more serious than that. Targeted too. Was Charlie having problems with anyone?"

Greg didn't answer straight away. He looked across the creek, picking at a tuft of grass by his leg. When he spoke, it seemed with some reluctance.

"I don't know for sure Rose. I have only been back full time for about seven months. I think there have been problems for more than a year, perhaps eighteen months. There is no proof it is kids. No proof it isn't. But I agree. It seems targeted.

"From what I know, Charlie was copping the worst of it. Think about it Rose. He was in his eighties, no son or grandson taking over. You weren't here much. Most would consider him an easy target. But Charlie was tough. And smart.

"There is the situation with the cattle. But I think that is part of a bigger plan. Jamie tells me it's a conspiracy theory, but I think I'm on to something." Greg stopped, looked at Rose. She nodded.

"Tell me. Perhaps Jamie and your Dad, and the locals, are too close. Perhaps it takes someone who has been away to more clearly read the clues."

Encouraged, Greg continued. "You're right. There are other

factors. Number one is the drought. We've been drought declared for three years. Most spear points and bores have dried up. Those who can afford it have gone deeper. There is water there, but it's not good. The two dams servicing the area are now under ten per cent capacity. Agricultural irrigation has been halted, it's only for urban use now to keep the towns in the district going. Only a few properties border the creek. It's spring fed, never dries up. It seems to disappear under the ground in places, but pops back up. It makes Charlie's place, your place, more valuable than gold.

"A lot of farmers have sold their stock. Some have even sold their breeders. So when it does rain, they are going to struggle to restock. Most farms, like yours, grow their own feed. Oats, hay, lucerne. This place is one of the few that can still irrigate their crops. A lot have failed. There are foreclosures. About three a week at the moment."

Rose was shocked. She had heard talk of this, seen some articles in the press too, but no one had put it so succinctly. Charlie must have been under a lot of pressure.

"Go on. What else?" Rose lightly touched Greg's arm, encouraging him to continue.

"Charlie had an old-fashioned set of values. But you know that don't you? He also sold stock, but kept his breeders. He grew fewer crops. Although he had access to the water, he cut his use back by at least fifty percent. Could be more. That's just a guess. He did that to ensure farmers downstream still had water."

Rose wiped a tear away as she nodded. Charlie had good values. Had instilled them in her. She thought in her father too, but perhaps something else had happened there. A question for another day.

"But why mess round with his cattle, letting them out? I still don't get it?"

"To make it hard for him. To make it hard for him to keep going. The second factor is the consortium working the area. Rosewood Beef have plans to build a massive feedlot in the region. Charlie's place, your place, is key to that. I believe that offers were made to Charlie as long ago as two years. If I'm right, the offers have been more frequent and higher, in recent months. Charlie resisted. He was saving the place for you. But I think he knew you would have to sell out, eventually. Perhaps his stubborn refusal was to drive the price up, give you a better deal. Who can say? Charlie's gone now. But Rose, you're here. You're a young woman alone. Your dog has been killed ..."

Greg lay back, a piece of grass between his teeth. Rose lay back beside him, thinking through his words. She sat up.

"And Ruff. Was killing Ruff part of the plan to frighten me? Convince me to sell? Who would do such a thing, kill an old dog like that ..."

Greg rolled on to his side, facing Rose. He took her hand. "There are rumours. Some say Angus Hamilton is working for the consortium and ingratiated himself with Charlie to wear him down. From what I saw at the party last night, now he is working on you. There is also talk that Douglas Barlow acts for them ..."

Rose sat up. Angus? And Douglas? Not possible. Or is it? It sounded plausible.

"I appreciate you telling me this Greg. Thank you. I will do some investigating myself. I've been on edge since the night Ruff died." She frowned. "How do you know he was killed? I told Debbie he passed away from old age." Rose drew back from Greg.

"Don't be alarmed. Sergeant Carrol, Nick, told me. He asked me to keep an eye out for any strange vehicles hanging around. I've been watching the place, as much as possible ..."

Relieved, Rose smiled at Greg. "Thank you. I appreciate that. You know, I like this side of you. Serious. Kind. Generous. You could do well to lose your smart-ass-football-star routine." She stood up and flicked her wet towel at him.

Greg laughed as he stood up. He caught the towel and pulled her closer. Leaning down, he kissed her quickly on the cheek. "I know I'm a dickhead when I have a few beers. Or rum. But Rose, I'd like to start over with you. Let me help you with this. Talk to me if you're worried about anything. Let me prove my worth."

Rose held her hand out to shake. "Friends. Old friends." Greg shook her hand and grinned at her. "That's all I ask. Friends is a good start."

NEXT MORNING, Rose showered and dressed, before heading down to the stables to feed the horses. Topper was moving freely and Rose studied the filly again as she came up for hay. She had a sound confirmation and looked a lot like her sire. Rose held out some hay for the young horse, trying to remember what her grandfather had called her. Storm? Yes, that was it. Stormy. She was born on a stormy night; she recalled.

Greg's words at the creek had unsettled her. Could Angus be working with Rosewood Beef? The timing was right. They had started poking around in the area about the same time that Angus had arrived. Coincidence? Was he really all he seemed, genuine nice guy? Or had he played Charlie? Now he had the stock and an option to buy the land in three years, he could afford to hold on. If she sold, he had first option. Would it go straight to the consortium then?

And Douglas Barlow? Really? That was a long bow.

Angus was coming for dinner tonight. Could she have this conversation with him? Could she ask about Melanie? Nothing had really happened between them, did she even have the right to ask about Melanie?

So many questions. Walking back to the house, Rose felt her mobile vibrate. Taking it from the back pocket of her shorts, she saw it was Debbie.

"Hi bride-to-be." Rose smiled into the phone.

"Hey matron-of-honour-of-sorts." Debbie chuckled in return.

"Did the clean-up go OK?"

"Yup. All done before breakfast as Jamie predicted. The boys took the trestles back to the CWA before lunch." Debbie hesitated.

"Is something wrong Deb?"

"No. Not really. Angus left his ute here. You know, after he drove Melanie home. She was pissed. Apparently she threw up before he could get her in her car. Anyway .... He came back for his car in the morning."

"And?"

"Melanie drove him. Jamie and I were at the woolshed, sorting through the engagement presents when they arrived."

"Are you trying to tell me something Deb?" Rose had a sick feeling in the pit of her stomach. She shouldn't care. He was nothing to her. He was worse than nothing. Maybe he was a sneaky dog-killing, cattle-rustling, property-stealing bastard.

But maybe he wasn't. Maybe he was a bail-an-old-man-out-of-his-mortgage good guy. Rose tuned back in to Debbie's words.

"Well. She was all over him. Melanie. Thanking him for driving her home and *staying over*. Tiffany gave him a hug good-bye, thanked him for breakfast. They seemed... I don't know. Close. Family-like. I've never really taken to Melanie but I hear she is a good mum and I've also heard she rarely gets plastered like she did last night. Maybe they have... a thing. Maybe she got drunk because he was showering you with attention." Debbie hesitated.

"I don't want you to get hurt Rose. I thought Angus was one of the good ones. But now. I don't know."

Rose clenched her teeth for a moment. "Thanks Debbie. I appreciate the heads up. I'm not sure about Angus either and with the complication of Charlie's will, it seems inappropriate to get involved, at the very least. Knowing this will keep me on message. He is coming for dinner tonight to talk about the will. It will be a business discussion. I don't plan to ask about his personal life."

"Stay strong Rose. Stay on message. Good luck." Debbie looked at Jamie as she ended the call. He raised his eyebrows.

"I know Angus, Debbie. He is a good bloke. I don't know what happened with Melanie last night but I really don't think they're involved. I don't think you should have meddled. Rose is a grownup. She can work it out."

Debbie put her arms around her fiancée. "She is my oldest friend. It's a sisterhood thing. We look out for each other. It's not meddling."

Jamie dropped a kiss on Debbie's forehead. "I hope you're right."

23

A ngus drove slowly out to Barrington after picking up a bottle of red wine. It annoyed him he had needed to drive Melanie home last night. It was not like her to get drunk like that. She was a good mum and to even consider getting behind the wheel with Tiffany in the car ...

It had been tough. Melanie had run straight to the bathroom, throwing up and crying. He had gotten Tiffany into bed. She had barely woken, so he had tucked her in fully clothed, only removing her little riding boots.

He sat in the bathroom with Melanie for over an hour, worried she would pass out and choke. Finally she stopped vomiting, but had wanted a shower before going to bed. Angus had drawn the line there, telling her to sort her own shower out and that he would take her car back to the clinic and return in the morning.

Melanie had cried and begged him to stay. Told him she wanted him. Tried to kiss him. Told him she would take sleeping tablets, which terrified him. He ended up sleeping on her sofa which was too short for his long legs and bloody uncomfortable.

He was embarrassed next morning when Melanie made a point of telling Jamie and Debbie he had stayed the night. But they knew him. They knew he wouldn't take advantage of a drunk woman. Yes, he had made a breakfast, of sorts. Melanie was sick and Tiffany was hungry. He had whipped up scrambled eggs on toast, about the only breakfast he could cook and made strong black coffee for Melanie, who hadn't been up to eating anything.

He hoped it would end there. That there would be no talk in town. Melanie was his employee. He didn't want it to get awkward or be forced to let her go. It would be unprofessional to be involved and while he thought Tiffany was a delight, Melanie was not at all his type. Too needy. Inclined toward possessiveness too, he'd wager money on that.

Now Rose Gordon was another situation entirely. Strong. Independent. Witty. Clever. Lover of horses and dogs. Sexy as hell. He liked her more every time he saw her. They had connected last night. Really connected. If it wasn't for Melanie, she may have asked him to follow her home. The possibility had been there. They both felt it.

He walked up the steps to Barrington, wine bottle in hand. It felt like a first date. Silly. But there it was. The large doors stood open, only the screen doors were closed. It was a warm night.

Rose came to the door as he was raising his hand to knock. She was dressed in a sleeveless shift in a rich cream colour, her hair in a messy bun on top of her head, making her seem taller, her feet bare. No make-up that he could determine, maybe some lip gloss. She looked understated and ravishing. He felt overdressed in good jeans and a collared shirt.

"Hey." She opened the door and took the bottle he held out to her. "Nice. Tyrrells Shiraz. Got to love those Hunter Valley wines. Thank you."

Rose asked Angus to pour the wine, while she bustled around, putting out pita bread, olives and dip. He was hoping she would ask about Melanie; he felt he needed to explain, but Rose did not mention Melanie, or even the party.

After an appreciative sip of her wine, Rose asked Angus what he knew about Rosewood Beef.

"Do you do any work for them Angus? I hear they have already bought the Andrews place and construction has begun."

Angus put his glass down and leant back a little. He considered Rose's question. "I understand they will have their own Vet full time once they are scaled up. I don't work for them and really don't want to have anything to do with them. However, I attended out there once, a few months ago. It was an emergency and no one else was available."

Rose nodded. Angus looked at her directly, let out a breath. "They made me an offer to be their Vet. Sell my practice and work full time with them. It was a very large offer.

"I thought about it. For less than a minute. Yes, private practice can be demanding and at times like this financially unrewarding. With the drought going on so long, many people pay slowly, if at all." He sighed. "I accept barter, mostly stock, which I started keeping out here. Charlie had sold some of his and still had feed, due to his access to water. In return I looked after his animals at no charge. It was a good arrangement, and we became friends. I knew what Charlie's reaction would be if I took the offer."

Angus stopped there, drank the rest of his wine in one gulp. "By that time I had come to look upon Charlie as.... Well....as more than a friend. Maybe a grandfather replacement. I'm a grown man and this may sound soppy, or needy. But I really, really liked Charlie. He put out the word that he was using my services in the beginning and a lot of the big family farms started using me too. A recommendation from Charlie was worth gold." Angus chuckled. "Maybe not gold. Maybe a mixture of beef and dairy stock, some lambs and a lot of home-cooked casseroles."

Rose smiled. She felt the sincerity of Angus' words. His friendship with Charlie had to be genuine.

"I told Charlie about the offer. He said my practice will turn around when the rains come. I know he is right. I just wish he had lived to see it. We talked about the feedlot. He told me he had been made an offer to sell the year before. He refused and made them deal through Douglas Barlow. Said he wouldn't speak with them directly. I think Douglas gives them the run around too. He and Charlie were solid mates."

Rose relaxed. Greg's conspiracy theory didn't hold water. Someone local may be working with the large company, but she doubted it was Angus or Douglas.

They chatted about the long range weather forecast while Rose cleared their snacks and returned with a delicious smelling lamb stew. Angus leant over the plate, almost planting his nose in the stew. "Hmmm. Smells familiar. Is this a Tait stew? Tait lamb?"

Delighted, Rose laughed out loud. "Yes. I was never going to be able to pass this off as my own cooking. It's one that Jill

Tait left in the freezer after the funeral. My own cooking style is less traditional. I enjoy throwing together a Thai stir-fry or something with seafood. Garlic Prawns are my specialty. Of course, living on Sydney Harbour helps. Access to seafood."

"Love garlic prawns myself. Do you throw any chilli in? I don't mind a bit of spice." Angus had lowered his voice slightly. It resonated with her. Rose felt a flush of warmth hit her face. Embarrassed she held her serviette to her mouth for a moment and reached for the wine bottle.

"Allow me." Angus poured the deeply hued wine into her glass, his eyes never leaving hers.

"Thank you." Rose needed to get back on track, this was not going to plan.

Rose drew a deep breath. "Chilli. Yes. But Angus, we need to talk about the will."

Twirling the wine in her glass before taking another sip, Rose hesitated. "I've been going through Charlie's account ledgers and I think I understand what happened here. Perhaps you can confirm my assumptions?"

Angus nodded, but did not immediately answer the question. "Your great-great-grandfather chose this land well, all those years ago. Good country with a permanent creek, good soil for pasture and crop," he said in appreciation.

"I know. I think I always took it for granted. It didn't come easy for them and I now realise how difficult it has been for my grandfather in recent times." Rose waited for him to answer her question.

Angus reached across the table, took her hand in his. "I had Charlie's confidence this last year or so, but I did not set out to influence him, particularly regarding his will. However, he was under pressure and did not want to be forced to sell the farm, certainly not in his lifetime, and not at all if you had plans to come back to it one day. Rose, if I had been able to I would have offered to buy him out, but that was beyond my finances. I could buy the stock, however. I believe that left the title free and clear."

Rose nibbled at her bottom lip. Should she ask if Angus knew anything about the mortgage, how it came about? Was it her own father's poor management or was it her fault, in accepting her inheritance without question?

Instead, she raised her glass in a toast and said "So here we are. I own the land."

Angus responded in kind, "Yes. Here we are. I hold the stock."

24

Rose cleared her throat, the intensity of her attraction to Angus sending her to her feet, almost knocking over the bottle of wine. Angus stood in the same moment, setting the teetering bottle to rights, firmly. Ducking her head a little, willing herself not to boldly meet his gaze, Rose began clearing the plates. Angus gathered up all but their glasses and the unfinished wine and followed her into the kitchen.

Setting the dishes in the sink, she turned to him. Looked at him, aware her eyes had darkened and her face was flushed. "Let's leave these. Can you top up our glasses? We can sit out back where it's cooler."

Angus raised his eyebrows but did as he was asked. Opening the screen door , Rose stepped out first, startling a large man standing in the dark under the tree where Ruff was buried. He took off noisily, running away from the homestead, through the orchard.

Rose screamed and dropped her glass off the edge of the veranda. Angus was already running after the intruder. He shouted back over his shoulder, "throw all the outside lights on Rose, quickly!"

Rose dashed inside and flicked the light switches for front and back. Angus had disappeared into the orchard where the light didn't reach. She waited anxiously, not sure if she should call the police. It had been too dark to get a look at the man, but she had registered that he was large and could move quickly.

Angus reappeared, breathing hard. "Did you get a look at him Rose?"

"No. It was too dark." She stepped down and walked toward the pear tree and Ruff's grave. Angus was walking around it, gazing from side to side.

Reaching the grave, Rose could see footsteps and scuff marks all over it. She shivered. Angus put his arm around her, drawing her close.

"Someone's been standing here, watching the house. And not just tonight. We need to let Sergeant Carroll know. It's likely the person who killed Ruff. This is not random or opportunistic. Someone is targeting you. Or Barrington. Or both."

Leaning against him slightly, she shivered. Angus tightened his arm around her, reassuringly. Returning inside, Rose made coffee while Angus put in a call to the police.

He hung up as she carried the tray out. "Do you want to sit in Charlie's study? It's private in there. Feels safer somehow. Are the police coming out?"

"No. They are attending an accident on the highway leading into town. Several cars and a truck. They'll send someone out tomorrow." Angus took the tray from Rose and walked into

Charlie's study, setting it down on the low table in front of the big leather couch.

They settled on the couch together. Close but not touching. Angus gave a half smile. "I've spent a few nights on this couch. Used to come out for a bite to eat with Charlie. We'd get talking over dinner, clean up, then he'd bring out a bottle of port. He'd tell me not to drive and that I needed to be out here early to check on the stock, anyway. Ha! He enjoyed a bit of company. Told a few good yarns too. Wouldn't surprise me if there was some truth in a lot of them."

Rose turned sideways, watching the emotions pass across Angus's face when he spoke of his friendship with her grandfather. The depth of his feelings for Charlie stirred her.

Passing her a coffee, Angus turned toward her and reached out, tugging at a wayward curl that had escaped her bun during the commotion.

Self-consciously, Rose lifted a hand to her hair, inadvertently causing more of it to come loose from the bun. "It was meant to be business-like. To help the conversation about the will."

"Business like? As opposed to what? Stunning? Desirable? Sexy?" He lowered his voice and moved closer. "I'm staying the night, by the way. I'm not leaving you here by yourself. Old mate out there may have circled back, be waiting for me to leave. I will not leave." Angus was firm.

Rose nodded. She didn't want to be here by herself either, there was every chance the prowler would come back. He leaned closer. She imagined she could feel a gravitational pull that drew her toward him. A few more inches and his lips would be on hers.

Before their lips came together, Rose jumped to her feet.

Get a grip girl, you can't fall at his feet like this. You still don't know what the Melanie situation is.

With a cheeky grin Rose grabbed the blanket from the back of the couch, tossing it to him. "Just as well you are familiar with the accommodation. This should keep you comfortable."

Angus choked back a mouthful of coffee. "Ok. Not what I was hoping for, but better than sleeping outside your bedroom door. For safety reasons, of course."

"Of course." Her smile slipped. She stepped closer to Angus, leant down and kissed him briefly on the lips. "I appreciate you staying. And perhaps there is more to talk about, between us. But I need answers first. I want to be sure I understand Charlie's reasons. I have questions about my parents, particularly my father, that I never asked when they were alive."

Rose gestured at the beautiful, if somewhat masculine, richly furnished room. "This house, this property, has defined me in many ways. But I feel the rug slipping beneath my feet. Somehow, not knowing my father's story has undermined my own. It's hard to explain."

Angus seemed about to reach for her, but withdrew his hand. "I understand. Take your time. I'm not going anywhere. At least, not tonight."

Nodding, Rose said good night and went to her room. She showered and put on an old tee shirt and boxer shorts, before sliding into bed.

Questions were playing on her mind. Was the mortgage caused by her father? His secret passion for flying? Or was it drought and poor farming conditions? Or did it begin when her parents died, to pay for her education and inheritance?

Closing her eyes, she wondered if she would sleep. Getting up, she checked her bedroom door to the veranda was locked.

In her mind's eye, she pictured Angus arriving, opening the front screen door. Did she lock it after dinner? They definitely locked the back door. No. She didn't think she had locked it.

Looking at the time on her phone, she realised she had been in bed for over an hour. Angus would be asleep. She would pop out and check the front door was locked.

With her phone in hand for muted light, she opened her door and listened. No sound. Angus must be asleep. Walking quietly past the study, she paused for a moment. The door was ajar, probably so he could hear her if needed. No snoring. She smiled to herself.

Into the hallway now, she walked quietly to the front door, avoiding the section where the floorboards creaked. Locked. She didn't remember doing it but perhaps Angus had after she went to bed. Good. All secure. Back to bed. She should be able to sleep now.

Tiptoeing past the study door, she paused again. She heard something. A little peek at him asleep wouldn't hurt. Pushing the door further open, she was about to step in when a movement behind made her spin around. Rose screamed.

Angus wrapped his arms around her quickly, holding her to him. "Shh. Sorry. I thought I heard something near the front door. Went to check. Didn't realise it was you until you spun around."

Her heart still racing Rose hiccupped back a sob. "It's ok. I was checking I had locked the front door. Thought you were asleep."

With his arms still around her, one hand rubbing the small of her back, Rose realised he was only wearing jeans. No shirt. The jeans weren't even buttoned. And she was pressed against him full length. In a tee shirt and boxers. His chest was hairy.

And hard. So were her nipples, pushed against him with very thin fabric between them. She knew she should step back, go back to bed. But the sensation of his arms holding her close, his hand rubbing her lower back, was mesmerising. She felt safe in his arms. And sexy. So sexy right now. Her body seemed to mould itself to his.

Angus murmured in her ear. "Just checking the door was locked? Really? Yet I came upon you sneaking into the study. Wanting to check if I snored?" A giggle escaped her. She started to move back, but he held her firmly.

"Oh. So that's it. You're not keen on a snorer? I don't know if I snore. Perhaps you should come in here with me, you might find out. Later." Angus started walking her backwards, still with his arms around her, into the study.

She wanted to stop. Truly. But when her knees hit the edge of the couch she sank down on it. Her arms were around his neck. How did they get there? Rose couldn't remember, but she drew him down with her. He had one foot on the floor and lowered his body, almost languidly, onto hers while he bent his head and kissed her. Just a nibble of her lips at first, then a little harder.

She wriggled under him and he took his mouth from hers. "Rose?" She knew what he was asking.

"Yes. Yes. Don't speak. Kiss me." It was all she could say. The intensity of the moment gripped her. She opened herself to his kiss and tried to get one hand between them, reach into his jeans. She could feel his erection against her thigh.

Taking his mouth from hers, Angus stood. In one quick movement he turned on a small table lamp and drew his jeans off. His nakedness was beautiful. Tall. Lean. Hard. A smattering of chest hair. Right then and there she decided she was not a fan of the metrosexual trend. Not a fan of men who wax. Standing over her was a man's man. Yep. She could get on board with that. With him. Definitely a man's man. Not a lot of them around.

Reaching down, Rose began to pull her tee shirt over her head.

25

Watching the play of emotions on her face, Angus attempted some self-talk. Stop now. She told you earlier she isn't ready. Needs answers, clarity. Do the right thing and put your pants on.

Lifting the shirt over her head, Angus saw her breasts and any thought of stopping left his consciousness as he gazed at them, round and full, nipples like tiny pebbles. She smiled lazily at him, then began to draw down her boxer shorts.

He took her hands from the waistband, replacing them with his own. Slowly, gently, inch by inch he pulled them over her flat belly, her hips. He saw her pudenda, just a tiny strip of auburn hair, and bent to plant a kiss, right there. The boxer shorts now on the floor, leaning over her he placed a knee between her legs, nudging them open.

Her mouth made an 'O' shape. They couldn't stop now. It felt good. It felt right. Kneeling above her for a moment he gazed down the long length of her. Broad shoulders for a woman. Tall. Long shapely legs. Nice bum. Round, not too big. Small waist. Full breasts. Firm. He placed a mouth over first one nipple, then the other, rewarded by a sigh from Rose, as she urged him closer.

Her heels were around his hips, feet on his bum. She was pulling him, soundlessly, closer. He paused. Wanted to draw out the moment. The first time. She is so beautiful. He put his lips to hers. She opened her mouth, kissed him back with unbridled passion.

Slowly, he entered her. Hot. Warm. Tight. She clenched around him. He would pace himself, make it last. He pushed all the way in and raised his head, looking into her eyes. Moving slowly at first, he built up a rhythm. Rose closed her eyes and let her head roll back, matching his thrusts with her own. Picking up pace he took a nipple in his mouth, gently rolling it between his teeth. She clutched him tighter, drummed her feet against his bum. Hell, if she kept that up it would be all over for him.

He flipped them over, Rose on top, riding him, back arched, head thrown back. He steadied her with his hands, holding her firmly at her hips. She leant down, crushing her breasts against his chest, still grinding her hips. Sexy as hell, this woman can go from zero to a hundred in moments. He watched the passion cross her face. Something primal about her. So cool and confident with her clothes on, hot and .... *abandoned* came to mind. She is able to just lose herself in the moment. That's a hell of a responsibility to hand a bloke. Giving him control. Ok then.

Wanting to slow himself down a little, he turned them on to their sides. Not a lot of room on the couch. Facing her, he slowed right down, stroked her hair, kissed her eyelids, nibbled on her bottom lip. He felt her relaxing; they were moving slowly together, making it last.

He waited until they were barely moving, looking into each other's eyes. She seemed slightly bemused, but made no move to stop.

Without warning, he flipped her on to her back and increased his pace. She opened her eyes wide and grabbed the back of his head pulling his mouth to hers. They ground their tongues together as he thrust harder until he felt her clench and shudder. Her moan in his mouth undid him and he thrust hard for a moment before giving himself up to her.

They lay together after, their hearts beginning to slow. He felt himself slip out of her. So beautiful. Gathering her in his arms, he bent his head, showering her with tender kisses. On her mouth, her eyelids, her hair, her cheeks. Her eyes were closed but a small smile played around the edges of her mouth.

His last thought, as he drifted off, wrapped around her on the old leather couch, was that he could really love a woman like this. He could really love this woman.

26

R ose moved and Angus opened his eyes, then smiled at her. It was a little uncomfortable on the couch; they were tall people. She kissed him on the mouth.

"Are we going to be awkward with each other today?" She nuzzled into his neck.

"I vote we don't, it's too delicious." He sat up, pulling her, still naked, onto his lap.

"Delicious? Mmmm, yes. Perhaps a shower though. What time do you open the clinic?"

Standing, Rose picked up her clothes, eyebrows arched at Angus.

Groaning, he reached for his watch. "Oh. It's only six. Don't open until eight. Time for a shower, breakfast and a quick check of the horses before I leave."

"Shower. Good." Rose began to walk from the room, still naked, exaggerating the swing of her hips as she did. He followed her.

"Um. Water restrictions. You know there is a drought on?"
she grinned cheekily over her shoulder.

"Yes. Very important to save water during the drought." He
caught up to her, steering her into the main bathroom.

Sᴇʀɢᴇᴀɴᴛ Cᴀʀʀᴏʟʟ and a constable arrived just as Angus was
leaving for work. They walked around the back with Angus and
Rose, who gave a brief run-down on the large size of the man
near the grave, and his bolt into the orchard and beyond.

Rose walked Angus out to his car while the police
photographed and measured the footprints on the grave. At the
car they paused. Angus touched her cheek. "I will be back
tonight. Around six. You're not staying here alone until we
know who is watching the house, and why."

"I have never imagined being afraid to be here alone at
night. I love this place, it's part of me. But there is someone
watching me, or the house. Either way, it's creepy. So thanks.
Please come back tonight. I'll whip up some stir-fry for dinner.
With chilli." She gave him a quick kiss.

Angus winked. "I'll be your protector. I may have to stay
very close to you to be sure you are safe."

Laughing, Rose opened his door. "Go now. There will be
talk."

He waved once as he drove out.

Sergeant Carroll moved toward her as she approached. The
constable was at the edge of the orchard taking photos.

"It's more worrying than we first thought Rose. The foot
prints are large, size 13. Angus wears a size twelve, so we can see
which are his. It looks like the intruder was here for some time

last night, lots of prints in the general area. There are others, a couple of days older, perhaps. Same shoes. It's also likely the same intruder that killed your old dog. I don't like you being here alone at night. It was good Angus could stay last night, but consider staying somewhere else for a night or two. Over at Tait's perhaps? I know they looked out for Charlie and that you know them well."

"It's ok. Angus said he will stay again tonight. We'll call straight away if we notice anything. Will try not to scare him off this time." Rose felt a slight blush stain her cheeks when she mentioned Angus staying over. The Sergeant didn't seem to notice.

The police gone, Rose walked down to the stables to feed the horses. They all came in; Topper was looking energetic. She stepped into the yard while he was eating and brushed him thoroughly. "You old fraud Topper. You used to scare me with your bad temper and snarly mouth, but you love a bit of attention, don't you?"

Storm, the filly, sniffed her hand when Rose reached out to her. Moving closer, quietly, she ran her hand down the filly's wither and along her back. Putting her arm under her neck, Rose patted her cheek, then held her by the halter and looked into her eyes. She had pretty eyes, gentle eyes. Good confirmation, strong legs. She would fill out more with good feed and some work.

On an impulse Rose selected a long lead rope from the stables and attached it to Storm's halter. With a handful of oats under her nose, Storm walked easily with Rose to the round yard. Rose walked around inside it, leading the horse by the halter, a few times each way. Rose let out three metres of lead rope and jogged clockwise, the filly trotting behind her. She lengthened the rope and moved to the centre, encouraging Storm to trot around the ring at the end of the rope. When Rose turned her anti-clockwise, Storm let out a small pig-root, kicking impatiently with her back legs.

Rose gently gathered up the excess lead rope and guided the horse toward her, speaking soothingly. "Well done Storm. Good girl. First time in the round yard for you. Let's take you back to the others and get some more oats, hey?"

Storm nuzzled the oats from her hand, back with the rest of the herd. Rose was pleased she had accomplished something with the young horse. She could almost hear Charlie's words. "Just take it slowly, you need to trust each other."

It's the same with people, she thought. Angus and I. We can take it slowly and learn to trust each other. Charlie trusted him, I should too. Perhaps this will work out. I can talk to my boss about working remotely a bit more. Maybe every second week. I could be here a couple of weeks each month. Train the filly, break her in myself. Get a puppy. Angus can move into my parents' quarters, so he has a space of his own. We can see where this might go, without forcing it.

27

Angus was late opening the small animal clinic. Three people were standing outside, two with dogs and one with something in a cat cage. Guinea pig? He couldn't see it properly as he opened the door and let them into the waiting room. Where was Melanie? She was usually here before eight, set up and ready to go.

Angus turned on the computer at reception, then sent a message to Melanie. *Are you unwell? Or Tiffany? Come in if you can, but if not, let me know you're ok.*

By nine he was running behind. No word from Melanie. He had seen a cat with a hairball, a guinea pig with diarrhoea, a pair of miniature poodles' for inoculations, cut the toenails of a great dane and told an elderly client that yes, her beloved pure-bred spaniel is definitely pregnant and no, he doesn't know who the father is. Glancing out at the waiting room, still full, he looked at the appointment list and called 'Mrs Anderson, please bring Percy through.' Mrs Anderson, grey, thin and wiry, came through to the surgery with her pet galah, Percy, in a cage.

Angus opened the cage, taking Percy out carefully. "And what seems to be the problem Percy?" The bird walked sideways along the surgery table. "Livin' the dream! Livin' the dream," the bird screeched. Angus grinned. He never tired of hearing the bird talk.

Mrs Anderson gave the bird a tickle on his neck. "His beak needs a tiny trim, he caught it on some wire in his big enclosure last night." She smiled at Angus. "He's got a new saying too."

Angus chuckled as he fetched his surgical instruments. Turning back to the bird he asked, "Still living the dream Perc?"

The bird repeated. "Livin' the dream. Livin' the dream." Then added "Help! They've turned me into a parrot, they've turned me into a parrot." Angus laughed, as he gently snipped the tiny jagged piece from the bird's beak.

His owner carefully put the bird back in his carry cage, then pulled a carton of eggs from her oversize tote bag. "Can you put that towards my account please Doctor Hamilton?"

Angus took the eggs, peeked inside. Free range, fresh this morning he was sure. "Paid in full Mrs Anderson, paid in full. I should pay Percy an appearance fee." Mrs Anderson nodded gratefully.

Following her back in to the waiting room, he saw Melanie was now at reception, busily checking arrivals against appointment times and dealing with the phone and invoicing at the same time.

Angus gave her a happy smile. She looked fine. A bit tired perhaps. All good. He could get on with his consultations, knowing she had the business end under control.

28

I t was almost noon when Rose dropped in to the café. Debbie came over with two coffees, sliding in next to her.

"I don't have long; the bank staff will be in soon. Lots of chai latte's and avocado salad."

"Sounds perfect. I'll have exactly that."

Debbie shook her head. "No. You're having a black coffee with a shot of caramel and a ploughman's lunch."

Rose laughed. "Do I have a choice?"

"Absolutely not. Now that we've sorted your lunch, how did it go last night with Angus?" Debbie looked anxious. "Did he explain about Melanie? Does he have something going there?"

Rose took a sip of her coffee, not looking at Debbie. "No. No, he didn't talk about Melanie. And I didn't ask. We talked about the will. Had a civilised dinner. Drank a bottle of shiraz...."

Debbie frowned. "Drank a bottle of shiraz? Really? You're not telling me something. I know you Rose Gordon. What else?"

Half a dozen customers in bank uniforms came in, sitting at the next table. Rose nudged Debbie. "You better get to work on those chai lattes' now. I will sit here quietly and await my ploughman's lunch."

Debbie jumped up, smiling at the customers, before turning around and saying, with some intensity, to Rose. "This conversation is not over."

Lunch was delicious. Rose was happy to wait, she could see the lunch rush was almost over and Debbie would be able to return for a quick chat. About to go to the counter to request another coffee, Rose saw Melanie rush in. She went straight to the counter. "Can I have Angus's lunch please?"

Cathy, one of Debbie's employees, handed a wrapped box to Melanie. "It's ready Mel. You're running later than normal?"

Melanie handed ten dollars to Cathy. "I was late in, Angus fell behind. All good, he's nearly done, but has to go straight out to the Wedge property to preg test some heifers after lunch." Rose stayed in her seat, watching the exchange. She noted that Melanie seemed to wince when she raised her arm to take the lunch from Cathy. Her sleeve fell back as she turned to go and Rose noticed a nasty bruise on her arm, just above the elbow. It looked like a handprint. Rose frowned. It looked sore and nasty. Melanie pulled her sleeve down quickly. She didn't see Rose.

Coffee in hand, Debbie came back to sit with Rose. "The rush is over. Tuesday's are quiet in the afternoon. I usually do a bit of bookwork out the back, then head home early. Cathy will close for me. I'm glad we don't do evenings."

"It's a big commitment, that's for sure. But it's yours Deb. I'm so in awe."

"Don't change the subject. We were talking about you and Angus and your dinner last night."

"We were? But that was a long time ago. I've had coffee and a ploughman's lunch since that conversation began."

"Tell."

"Dinner was great, the conversation was frank, I think. I learned more about him and his relationship with Charlie. I believe it was genuine." Rose was enjoying spinning the story, just a little, to get Debbie's reaction.

"And after dinner. How did you leave it?"

"After Angus called the police to report an intruder …"

"What? What intruder? What happened?" Debbie raised her voice.

"Ssh. Voice down. Yes, there was an intruder. It's not the first time either. I didn't want to tell you before the engagement party, you had enough to deal with. Whoever it is, was there during the week too. Ruff ran at him, protecting me. The bastard hit him hard, on the head …." Rose stopped, pulled a serviette toward her, swiping away a tear. "I'm so angry. That's how Ruff died. Angus couldn't help him."

"Bloody hell, Rose. You should have told me. I know you loved Ruff, he was such a big part of Charlie's life too. And last night, what happened? Did you get a look at him? It is a 'him', I assume?" Debbie put her arm around Rose's shoulders, squeezed, then let go.

"No. I didn't see much the first night. A large man perhaps. It was dark. Last night too. We walked out on the back deck with our wine, after dinner. We heard a branch break, then someone running. Angus took off after him, but once he reached the orchard, it was too dark. He could have gone in any direction. He was standing on Ruff's grave under the ornamental pear, you saw it on Wednesday night." Rose wiped away another tear. "He's been watching me. For days. Since the funeral at least. Watching me. Or the house. Or both. It's creepy."

Rose sat up straighter. "The police are patrolling during the night, down the side road too. They've told the neighbours to keep an eye out. I think Sergeant Carroll has already spoken to Greg. Greg spoke to me at the creek yesterday, he was checking from the other side on his bike."

"Good. I'll talk to Jamie, although Greg has most likely told him. Why didn't you come to me last night after it happened? You shouldn't stay there by yourself!"

"Um. Angus stayed. He didn't want me to be there by myself either. He slept on the couch in Charlie's study." Rose fiddled with her coffee cup.

Debbie tapped Rose on the shoulder, wanting to see her expression. "Really? The couch? All night?"

"Yes. All night."

Debbie drummed her fingers on the table. "You're leaving something out Rose. I know you." She put her hand to her chin, thinking, then turned back to Rose, her eyes narrowed slightly. "And you Rose. Where did you spend the night?"

Rose mumbled something. Debbie leaned in closer. Rose looked up, defiantly. "On the couch. I was on the bloody couch too! Are you happy now?"

Debbie crossed her arms. "Oh ... I'm happy if you are. No talk of Melanie? No clarity? But you slept with him?"

"Yes. And in the shower this morning, if you want all the saucy details." Challenge in Rose's tone.

Debbie hesitated. "I am happy for you. I've always liked Angus. Maybe there is nothing to the Melanie thing. It didn't look right, so I mentioned it. But you are adults, you can talk it through." More intensely, she said "Rose, you need to talk it through, to be sure."

"I know." Rose stood up, smiled quickly at Debbie. "That's why he is staying again tonight." Walking to the counter, she nodded at Cathy and passed over her card. Cathy looked past Rose to Debbie.

"Take her money Cathy. She's a big girl. So she tells me." Debbie laughed, nudging Rose as she walked by. "Another girl's night Rose. This week. We need to talk."

Sergeant Carroll called Rose on her mobile as she walked to the car. The Andrews family had made similar reports of a stalker or trespasser at their place two months ago. It was one factor that helped them decide to sell out to Rosewood Beef. Cattle had been released, several working dogs baited and the tap on a diesel bowser was left on overnight, emptying the tank by sun up. George Andrews had talked to his family; his wife, son and daughter-in-law, and they had decided together that selling was better than struggling through the drought, getting further in debt to feed the stock and keep the place running. George and Irene were ready to retire, they would move to the coast to be nearer their daughter and grandchildren. George Junior, locals call him Young George, was keen to start a specialty welding and engineering business and the sale gave him the capital to do it.

Rose asked if the Andrews family had sighted anyone, or if the police had taken fingerprints or had any leads. Sergeant Carroll advised there were no prints and no leads. They had really thought it was kids. A group of teenage boys, still at school, had taken to driving unregistered farm vehicles about at night, doing a spot of rabbit and roo shooting and making mischief. They had been hauled in to the station and questioned, but had emphatically denied it was them. Their parents had been adamant they were at home on those nights, but the police had been suspicious. Sergeant Carroll ended the call advising Rose not to stay in the homestead alone.

Pleased that Angus would stay, at least tonight, made Rose feel easier, but it was not a long-term answer. He would definitely need to move in before she returned to work, so the homestead was protected. What if the person lit a fire? Rose couldn't bear thinking about it.

Home again after picking up all she needed to make dinner, Rose spent a happy couple of hours in the round yard with Storm. She understood what to do now as Rose lunged her, first one way then the other, encouraging her to walk, trot and canter in turn. The filly was bright and interested and Rose thought she would try to 'mouth' her tomorrow, use a bridle with a light bit instead of a halter, lunge her on long reins for a few days. She would come down tomorrow and clean the bridle and long reins, they seemed stiff from lack of use.

Rose gave Storm a handful of oats and a brisk rubdown before releasing her back in to the horse paddock. She watched as Topper and the mares came up to greet her. Sitting on the fence, Rose realised she was due back at work in a week. Somehow, the thought of returning to work and her lovely apartment did not bring a smile to her lips, as it usually did. She felt settled here, despite the trauma of Topper's health and losing Ruff. She shook her head, mentally chastising herself. Could she have it all? Her career and apartment in Sydney and the homestead and farm?

Once back inside, Rose checked the time. Just after four, and Angus should be here around five, unless called to an emergency. She didn't have to prep for dinner; it was just a few vegetables and chicken for a satay chilli stir fry. Rose chuckled to herself. She didn't mind a bit of heat herself, let's see how Angus likes it.

Opening the door to her grandparents' room seemed slightly disrespectful. She had rarely come into their bedroom and hesitated in the doorway for a moment. The bed had been stripped, the mattress was bare. Glancing around, her loss hit her again. She had come to terms with her parents passing years ago, but her grandparents had been larger than life, timeless. They had always been here, a part of the homestead and the farm. Driving up for Charlie's funeral she had wondered if she would feel the same attachment for the place. Nodding to herself, she realised that it was more than just people, this place held her history, her family's history. She couldn't imagine her life without it.

Moving to the large rosewood chest at the foot of the bed, Rose let the tears fall as she knelt before it. Opening the lid, she saw several large photo albums, and reached in for them.

29

R ose didn't answer his knock on the front door. Glancing toward the stables, he could determine no activity there. Concerned now, Angus pushed the door open and went looking for her, a knot of worry in his chest. She really should lock the door when she is home alone, even during the day. He called out her name.

"In here." Rose's voice sounded different. Husky perhaps. Maybe she was waiting in her bedroom for him. Nice thought.

The door to Charlie's bedroom was ajar. Rose was on the floor beside the open chest, a photo album on her lap and tears running unchecked down her cheeks. His earlier thoughts vanished as he sat on the floor beside her. Rose pushed the album into his hands wordlessly. He held it in one hand, using the other to pull her close to him, kissing the top of her head.

He looked at the large photo in the album. Rose looked about fourteen and Ruff was a puppy, sitting beside Charlie's chair on the back veranda, his head cocked to one side. Rose was on the floor, her back against her grandfather's legs, a book in her hands. Charlie had his pipe in his mouth, his head inclined toward his granddaughter. It looked like she was reading aloud.

Sniffing, Rose said "I remember this. It was such a warm night that we sat on the veranda until late. We had been talking about Ruff and his training, and Charlie said that it made him think of Banjo Paterson poems. I fetched his leather-bound copy of the Complete Works of Banjo Paterson from the study. Gran was there; with the camera. I read to them. The Geebung Polo Club, Clancy of the Overflow and finished with The Man from Snowy River. It was such a perfect moment in time. When I finished, Charlie had this look on his face. He gave me a nudge with his foot and just said 'Off to bed with you,' but he'd loved it. I knew that."

His voice low, Angus said "I know that book well. Charlie would sometimes read a verse or two after a few glasses of port. He could recite The Geebung Polo Club without referring to the book. It's a lovely memory Rose. You should take some time to remember what this place, this home means to you. You had a very special childhood, growing up here." Angus set the album on the floor and put both arms around Rose, kissing her forehead and rocking her slightly.

"You're right. Charlie understood. He made his will the way he did to help me hang on to the place, and to give me time to decide if I want to live here myself. I've been thinking about it this afternoon. It's complicated."

"It is. But there is no rush." Angus stood. Reaching down, he took Rose's hands in his own, helping her to her feet.

"I will leave it like this," she gestured to the open chest, the albums on the surrounding floor. The chest was still three quarters full. "I'll leave the bedroom door open too. Then I can just pop in when I have a minute and explore a little more."

Happy to see her smiling, Angus pulled her into his arms and held her close. His earlier thoughts had completely dissipated. After a few moments, he looked down at her. "How about we open a bottle of wine? Can I do anything to help you with dinner?"

"Dinner is sorted. I'll open the wine." She stepped back and took him in. Still in his work clothes, he had indeterminate stains on his shirt and what looked like dry manure on one leg of his pants.

Glancing down at himself, he smiled wryly. "Mind if I have a shower and change? I'll be quick."

"Take your time. I'll open the wine. Dinner won't take long, but it's early yet." Her words were spoken brightly, but he felt an undercurrent of something in them. Dinner, shower, staying the night. It smacked of domesticity. Did it bother her a little? It was too soon to discuss their personal hopes for the future. Through Charlie's will and the threat of the trespasser, they had been thrown together, faster than their relationship would have developed in normal circumstances. He picked his bag up from the hallway and headed for the shower.

STANDING with the warm water soothing his muscles, his thoughts of Rose stirred him. There were decisions and choices she would need to make. He was beginning to hope she would choose to stay, or at the very least, return from Sydney more frequently, so they could take the time to get to know each other, work out what it is between them. Could they have a future together?

He was unprepared when Rose slipped in beside him, naked, a glass of wine in each hand, held away from the stream of water.

"Some wine after your hard day at work, dear?"

Playing along, he took a glass from her, chugging half in one big mouthful. "Thank you darling, but whatever have you done with your clothes?"

"Oh, I didn't want to get them wet." She raised her glass and downed the lot in three gulps.

Finishing his wine, he placed both glasses out on the bench beside the basin, then pulled her back into the shower with him. Dinner could wait.

Rose was preparing dinner, her still-wet hair tied in a loose ponytail making the back of her blouse damp. She took a sip from her glass as Angus came in off the back deck, wearing a dark tee shirt and faded cargo shorts.

"It's almost dark out there. No sign of anyone around and I've locked up. We can go out the back after dinner if you like, but I want to ensure no one can get in if we're distracted." He picked up the wine bottle, looked at it for a moment, raised an eyebrow to Rose in question.

"A top up please, don't overdo it. I need to keep my mind on the job at hand." Rose swept a small mound of finely cut vegetables and chicken into a hot wok. Turning back to Angus, brandishing a wooden spoon, she added "Distracted? What could possibly distract us?"

"Minx." Angus topped up his own glass and carried it to the table. Taking the cutlery Rose handed him, he set two places, folding napkins at the side of each setting.

"Hmmm, nice touch. I wasn't sure if you were a domestic beast, or a little on the wild side." Rose scraped what looked like red chilli into the wok, stirring it quickly. The smell was delicious.

Angus stepped close, his body hard against hers, her back against the kitchen bench. He wrapped one arm around her back, letting the other hand drop to the curve of her bum, holding her firmly. Leaning down until his mouth just brushed her lips, he growled, "Part beast, part house-trained. Be careful what you wish for."

30

Wiping his mouth with the serviette, Angus leant back in his chair and raised his glass to Rose. "Wonderful dinner, thank you. Just the right touch of satay and chilli. Love the peanuts tossed through too."

"My pleasure. I used more chilli than usual, but it worked." Rose flushed slightly, unused to such praise and possibly from the effects of the wine. They had opened a second bottle of Tyrrells Semillon Sauvignon Blanc, its crispness a perfect pairing with the Asian flavours of the meal.

Over dinner they discussed the terms of the will in practical terms. Angus acknowledged he would like to move into the homestead, sooner rather than later. His immediate concern was to provide a presence while Rose was there. She advised Angus she needed to be at work in Sydney on Monday, which meant leaving early Sunday morning at the latest.

They'd agreed Angus should take over her parents' quarters, providing some privacy and space of his own. Although they didn't discuss it, they knew they would spend the nights together in her room while she remained there.

Still chatting, they cleared the table. Angus washed up while Rose dried and put away the dishes.

"Your new digs have a kitchenette, but not a full kitchen. It's OK for making coffee and toast and quick snacks, but please use this kitchen as much as you want whether I am here or not. In fact, use the whole house." Rose put away the wok, conscious that Angus was now leaning against the sink, watching her. She blushed.

"Thank you Rose. I mean that. Being able to move out here will give me some respite from the clinic. Folk know I live there, so I'm often interrupted out of hours for so-called emergencies, that under other circumstances could have waited until business hours." He hesitated for a moment. "I have a few things stored up the coast in Mum's garage, so I would like to bring some of them down here, if you don't mind." He caught her hand and pulled her close to him, casually linking his hands behind her back.

Without hesitation Rose responded, beaming. "Of course. You should make yourself at home." Blinking as he gently kissed the tip of her nose, she added teasingly. "I'm curious though. What things do you want to bring here?"

"Books, mostly agriculture and animal husbandry textbooks that belonged to my grandfather." Angus paused. "I've kept a lovely old roll-top desk of my grandmothers that mum wanted to take to the tip. It needs a bit of restorative work, but maybe during the colder months I can strip it back and re-polish it. It's beautiful, and I'd like to use it as a personal desk, of sorts." Rose enjoyed watching the emotion cross his face as he spoke. His love for his grandparents was real and obvious and she liked that he spoke so freely of them, to her. "There is a chest of drawers, solid timber, also old, but I'm not sure how much I can fit in the space. I've never been in that part of the house. I think Vera closed it up years ago and Charlie never seemed to go in there."

Rose stepped away briskly, startling him. "Of course you haven't! You need to see it! We'll do it now." Tugging his hand, she pulled Angus along in her wake as she almost ran through the house, down the long hallway and out to the back veranda where a covered walkway led to the adjoining section that had been her parents' home.

Opening the door, Rose switched the light on, expecting to feel some sense of her parents. A hint of her mother's perfume, perhaps. But it was empty of anything she attached to her mother or father and everything was coated with a fine layer of dust.

The living area was roomy, with a wood-fired heater set into the original fireplace. The floors were hardwood boards, like the main house, and the ceilings high. The walls had shadows in a few places where pictures had hung. They were in her Kirribilli apartment now, along with the two sofas and side tables and a lovely standing lamp. The room was empty apart from a rug rolled up against one wall.

Angus followed her through to the bedroom. Empty except for the timber-framed queen size bed and a bare mattress. There were built in cupboards with hanging space, but no drawers. Angus could use the chest he had in storage. Looking at the bed, she turned to Angus.

"Would you use this, or bring yours in from the clinic?" He seemed to hesitate for the moment.

"Keeping one at the clinic is handy, especially if I get a

locum from time to time or need to sleep there to monitor a patient. But I can replace this if you would rather I didn't use it." He waited, while Rose turned in a circle, looking around the room. She seemed to decide.

"Use it. The whole place seems devoid of anything that is special to me. Their personal things are in the pair of chests in the main house. I have most of their furniture, and paintings, in my place in Sydney."

Pleased with her decision, Rose walked through the small study, which had been her nursery when she was very young, to the kitchenette.

Opening the few cupboards, she noted there was a dinner service and cutlery and basic cooking utensils, although there was only a two burner cooktop and microwave oven. A kettle and toaster remained, and a refrigerator, standing with the door ajar. It had been turned off for many years.

Rose reached behind and turned it on. It began to hum quietly. "I will give everything a spring clean tomorrow, open the windows and air it out and check all the appliances work. You can bring your stuff in any time you like. I will get you a key. I think this building is keyed separately, but I will dig up a full set, including the house, for you."

"What do you think? Will it do?" Rose turned to Angus.

He tucked his arm around her. "It's perfect. The rooms are generous, and so are you, to allow me to use this space as my own. It's just right for the few pieces I have stored, although I may need to buy a sofa or chairs for the living area." Turning her to face him, he planted a gentle kiss on her lips.

Lifting her arms, she draped them around his neck and pulled him closer, kissing him back. There was no urgency or passion in either kiss, but it felt like a commitment of sorts had been made. Share the house, get to know each other, see where it went. To Rose, it felt like a beginning. It felt great and a little fission of happiness bubbled up until she let out a small chuckle.

He felt it too, she could tell by the gentleness of his touch, the look in his eyes. Pulling back, she said, "But wait, you haven't seen the best room yet."

Raising his eyebrows, he repeated "Best room?"

On the other side of the main bedroom which was in the building's corner with a veranda on two sides, stood a door. Rose strolled over, Angus behind her, and threw it open to reveal a stunning bathroom. Large black-and-white tiles spanned the floor, checkerboard style, setting off the enormous white claw-foot bathtub in the centre of the room. Angus glanced around, wonderingly, at the bath, large shower and the basin set into a timber bench top. A linen press created a divide, behind which the toilet crouched, glossy white.

"Wow! Great bathroom!" He turned, taking it all in.

Rose perched on the edge of the bath, memories taking her breath. For a moment she thought she would cry, but gathered herself. "When Mum was ill, she liked to take a bath, it helped ease her pain. At the time, they had only a shower, toilet and basin in a much smaller space. Dad and Charlie renovated, pushed further out onto the veranda, and quickly. We knew she was terminal, but they wanted her to be comfortable and able to stay in her own space as long as possible. They needed to make the shower big enough for a chair, so it made sense to do it properly.

"In her last weeks, I came home and stayed until the end. We spent a lot of time in here, Mum and I. She would lie in the bath, with her bubbles and scented soap and we would talk. I had never really felt close to my parents, but in those last weeks it was as if Mum was trying to make up for that, and perhaps for the times we would never share together. Sometimes I would read to her. She told me of the dreams she had for my life...we had never spoken to each other like this before." A tear escaped and Angus sat beside her, holding her hands, giving her time to gather her thoughts.

Looking up at Angus, her lashes damp, Rose tried to force a smile. "I haven't thought about those conversations since she died. I think I put it all away, somewhere deep down. I need to take some time. Remember her. Think about our long conversations."

Leaning her head on his shoulder, she could feel Angus rubbing her back, in small circles like you would for a crying child. His gentleness and the motion soothed her.

Standing again, they walked to the door of the bathroom. Before closing the door, Rose said "Would you mind if I come in here sometimes? I think I'd like to take a bubble bath and revisit the memories I have of Mum."

"Anytime you like Rose, anytime."

They sauntered through the rooms and found themselves back in the main house. At the door to her own room, Rose breathed, "I'm tired. It's been a big day. There are still things we need to discuss, but right now, I'm keen to sleep." Angus nodded, looked to step away.

Rose did not release his hand. "Stay with me Angus. Sleep with me tonight. I would like to try simply sleeping with you."

He nodded, kissed her gently, disengaged his hand. "I'm getting my bag from the hallway. I will do a last check that everything is locked up. Get ready for bed, I'll be back in a few minutes."

Nodding happily, Rose did just that. Angus returned, climbed into bed wearing a pair of boxers. He took her in his arms, kissed her gently. He had taken the time to brush his teeth. Nice. She turned on to her side, her back to Angus. He settled in behind her, wrapped around her. She drifted off. Safe. Happy.

31

A persistent beeping, and Angus cussing quietly in the dark, woke her. Turning on the side lamp, she saw Angus had his phone in his hand, the sheet already thrown back.

"What time is it? What's happing?" Fully awake now, Rose sat up.

"Sorry, it's almost two. The alarm at the clinic has been activated. It beeps me directly. I will have to head in, check it out." Standing now, he pulled on his clothes from the previous night.

"A break in? What do people want from a vet surgery?" Rose frowned.

"Drugs." Angus sounded grim. "Some are so desperate; they try to cook their own out of animal drugs. Having said that, the alarm can be sensitive, so it may be nothing. It happens."

"Do you want me to come with you?" Rose got out of bed.

Angus came around to her side, quickly, drawing her into a fierce bear hug. "No. Stay here. Go back to sleep. I will call the police if it looks like someone is inside. Otherwise I will just check everything is OK, re-set the alarm and come back." He had his wallet and keys in his hand before she had settled back into bed. She closed her eyes, sinking into her pillow, as he rushed out.

Driving into town, Angus swore under his breath. Such a great night with Rose, he had really wanted to wake up with her, make breakfast together. Face it mate, you're falling for her. She is everything Charlie said and more.

Slowing as he reached the urban speed limit he thought for a moment about the glimmer of vulnerability Rose had displayed when she spoke of her last conversations with her mother. She hasn't processed that. She needs to and it might bring up more stuff for her. Be prepared for that. And be there for her. She has no family. I think people around here forget that; she appears so strong and independent. Be a friend first.

Still self-talking, Angus pulled in to the back of the clinic, rolling in with the lights and the engine off for the last few metres. He could see there was a light on inside, although it looked like it was in his flat, rather than the clinic itself.

Quietly, he walked to the door, putting his ear against it. Whoever was in there had disabled the alarm. Kids? Someone looking for drugs, or money? He stepped back and dialled the police station, getting voicemail. As in many small towns, there was usually only one officer on during week nights, who may already be out on a call. He left a brief message.

Stepping back to the door, he tried it. It was locked. He slowly, quietly, unlocked it.

The door opened into a small room between the clinic and the flat, that Angus used as a laundry room. Standing there, listening, he could hear faint sounds from the flat, but the clinic was quiet. He picked up a golf club from his bag in the corner.

Tossing up whether he should back off and wait for the police, he heard what sounded like a sob. Again. It definitely sounded like a sob. A woman's sob.

Turning the doorknob slowly, he quietly opened the door to the flat. A bedside lamp was on, but it was still dim. There was a shape lying on the bed. No, IN the bed. What the hell? A woman, crying, in HIS bed. He reached for the main light switch, just inside the door.

"Melanie!" Shocked, Angus stayed by the door as Melanie sat up, hair tousled, face tear-stained. Frowning, he crossed his arms, waiting for a response.

Melanie looked down, not meeting his eye. She mumbled something, sobbing between words.

He couldn't make out what she said, but her misery and embarrassment was plain in her slumped posture, tangled hair, tear-streaked face.

Speaking softly, Angus took a step closer to the bed. "What is it Melanie, why are you here? Where is Tiffany?"

Seeming to pull herself together somewhat, she straightened her shoulders and tossed her hair back, and he saw at once the large bruise across the corner of her eye and down her jawline.

"Jesus Mel, who did this to you?" Concerned, Angus strode to the bed, sat on the edge and gently put his hand under her chin, turning her face to the light. Her mouth and jaw were bruised and swollen and he saw more bruises on her upper arms.

Melanie shook her head. "I can't tell you. I'm too embarrassed. Tiffany is at Mum's, but I couldn't go there. Couldn't let her see me like this. Don't make me leave, Angus, I need a place to stay tonight."

"I've left a message with the police Mel, they may turn up at any moment. You set the alarm off."

"I ... I know. I was rushing, couldn't get the code punched in quickly enough." She looked sadly up at Angus.

"Whoever did this to you Mel .... " he stopped, took a breath. "You need to tell the Police, you've been assaulted. You need help. You should tell your Mum ..."

Melanie started sobbing and yelling "No. No. No. No one. Tell no one!" she was shaking, clutching the sheet to her chest terrified. Angus stood up abruptly, realizing she had on only a bra.

"Please Angus, I beg you. Don't tell anyone. Please!" Moved by her desperation and near hysteria, he nodded.

"All right Mel. I will leave another message; tell them it was a false alarm. You're safe here." Angus walked into the clinic, checking all was OK there, while he re-dialled the police station. There was no sign anyone had been in the clinic at all. Leaving a message, he returned to the flat.

Still sitting up in bed, sobbing quietly, she looked at him fearfully. Standing by the bed, he spoke gently, "I've left a message at the station that everything is in order here. But Melanie, it will be obvious tomorrow that you're hurt. You really need to get some help. I'd like to take you up to the hospital now, have them check you out."

With her head in her hands, she moaned softly, then looked up at Angus. "No Angus. Please. Let me handle this. I just need some sleep and to use your bathroom to clean up later. I will take a few days off, head to Sydney, see a doctor there. I can leave Tiff with Mum. I was taking leave anyway. You know what this town is like, I can't let anyone see me. I need to protect Tiffany." Her voice seemed stronger, determined.

Sighing, he nodded. "OK Melanie. I'll head back to Barrington now. Just promise you will see a doctor. Is ... is it someone local that did this to you?"

Shaking her head, Melanie clamped her lips together. "I'll never say. Don't ask me Angus. I will never, ever say."

"Then this person gets away with this Melanie. If you don't report it, they will never be punished.

"I just can't. Don't ask me."

Sighing, Angus moved toward the door. "Can I get you anything before I go? A cup of tea? There is Panadol in the kitchen ...."

"Thanks Angus. I'll be OK." Relieved, she laid her head back on the pillow, keeping the covers to her chin. "Can you ... can you please lock up securely when you leave? I'm sure I'm safe here, but ..."

"Sure. Get some sleep Mel."

Quietly closing the door behind him, Angus paused outside. What did she mean she's sure she's safe? Could the bastard that did this to her come looking for her here? Is it her ex-partner, Tiffany's father? I never heard her say he was violent or abusive, just that they were young and it didn't work out. It's the only explanation really, why she wouldn't report it, not wanting Tiffany's Dad to be charged, or worse. Could that be it?

Walking in to the clinic, Angus noted it was almost four am. No point going back to Barrington now. Should he message Rose? He didn't want to wake her up. What could he tell her? False alarm. It was a lie, but he had promised Melanie. It weighed heavily on him after the pleasure of being with Rose the night before, glimpsing a future full of possibility.

32

Waking at five, Rose saw Angus had not returned. She sent a quick text.

Everything OK?

He messaged back. *False alarm. Didn't want to wake you a second time.*

Ok. Want to come back for breakfast?

Smiling, Rose took her phone to the kitchen, filled the kettle and opened the fridge. Omelette, she decided. That would do the trick. Angus may want to have a quick shower and change, then breakfast, before he starts his day. She glanced at her phone. No reply. He is probably already driving back.

Ten minutes passed, Rose had showered quickly and made a pot of tea. Her phone beeped.

Sorry Rose. Busy day, will take advantage of the early start.

Disappointed, Rose poured herself a black tea, adding a teaspoon of honey and stirring. No problem, she will feed the horses and work the filly for a while. Perhaps a quick trip to town for coffee with Debbie, then home to clean her parents' part of the house so Angus can move his things in whenever he was ready. Good plan. If she had time, she would look through the rest of both chests, see what else she could find.

ROSE PARKED near the café just before noon. It was busy; she wondered if Deb would have time for a chat. A brightly coloured tourist bus pulled up in front of her, spilling out a small group of young people who promptly entered the café. Hmmm, Deb would definitely be busy. Maybe she should call in at the clinic, see if Angus had time for lunch together.

Walking into the clinic, she smiled at Angus as he walked an elderly lady carrying a cat cage to the door. He was surprised to see her, and she saw he had two patients left in the waiting room.

"Hi. Thought you might be ready for a lunch break, but I can see you have patients waiting ..." Rose raised her eyebrows a little. Looking toward the reception desk, she noted it was empty. "Is Melanie in the surgery?"

Angus looked at her for a moment, then blurted, "Melanie has taken early leave. I'm on my own today. I have young Freddie Campbell coming from Monday for two weeks, so it's just small animal clinic today and Friday morning that I'll be a bit pushed." He cocked an eyebrow at her cheekily. "If you are keen to give me a hand, I'll finish quicker."

"Seriously?"

"Sure. Madison over there needs to have stitches removed." He nodded at the small white Shitsu sitting in the lap of a large grey-haired woman, patting her pet nervously. "If you could hold her for me, Miss Grayson can stay in the waiting room."

"Ok." Slightly surprised, but a genuine lover of dogs, Rose smiled at Miss Grayson, taking Madison from her arms and followed Angus into the surgery.

"Scrub up over the sink. Use the brush and the disinfect wash. Then pop on the apron there, and fresh gloves, over here." Angus took the trembling dog from Rose and she did as she was asked. Watching him from the corner of her eye she noted he was gently soothing the small dog, speaking softly, while he examined her wound.

With apron and gloves on she stepped over to the stainless steel bench, looking expectantly at Angus.

Continuing to speak quietly, he said "Madison, this is Rose. Rose, this is Madison. She tore her shoulder trying to escape under a fence while fleeing from a large cat."

Using a similar tone, Rose place her hands gently on the small dog and soothed "Hello Madison, that's a nasty cut you have there. Looks like you have about eight stitches to come out. I hear Doctor Hamilton is very, very good at removing stitches."

"Hold her here, and here Rose." Angus showed her where to put her hands. He swabbed the shaved patch on the little dog's shoulder, then began to gently remove the stitches, speaking as he worked. "Miss Grayson was almost hysterical when she brought her in just over a week ago. She has been warring with her neighbour about that darn cat for years. It's twice the size of Madison, but she is a feisty little thing and insists on chasing it. She dug a hole and got into the neighbour's yard, then the cat arked up and chased her out. She caught herself on the bottom of a broken railing."

"Poor girl." Rose murmured to the little dog, still shaking, but otherwise making no noise.

Angus continued. "Sometimes I get the owners to come in for small surgeries like this, it can often help keep their animal calm, but I'm afraid Miss Grayson is easily upset, so this is a much better option." The stitches out, he swabbed again, then bandaged the area. "There you go Madison. As good as new. Keep away from that big old tabby cat now."

Angus opened the door to the waiting room. Rose removed her gloves and carried the small dog out, gently placing her in her owner's arms. "She did very well Miss Grayson. Vet says to come back on Friday and he will check the wound and change the bandage. You can sort the fees out then." She understood the attachment the woman felt for her pet, Rose had been the same about Ruff.

Angus had called in the last patient, a wriggling Labrador pup, and put the closed sign on the front door. "This won't take long Rose, just some shots for young Harry. George will hold him for me." George was a sprightly looking gentleman of indeterminate years who looked more than capable of holding his puppy while he had his needles.

"Throw that apron in the laundry, in that little room between the office and the flat. Won't be long, we can walk down to the cafe for a quick lunch."

Rose went through to the laundry, removing the apron and placing it in the hamper. It was half full, and she contemplated putting a load in the machine in the corner, then decided it would be overstepping.

The door to the flat was ajar, so she peeked in. The bed was unmade; Angus must have tried to get a couple of hours' sleep when he came in to check the alarm. Hearing him still chatting with George in the surgery, she decided to go in and make the bed for him quickly.

Pulling the sheet up she noticed a small spot of blood on the pillow slip. Odd. She hadn't noticed Angus had a scratch on his face or neck. Looking closer, she saw two long blonde hairs, one on the pillow and the other on the sheet. Blonde hair like Melanie's.

Leaving the bed half made, she backed out of the room and closed the door, heart racing. What the hell? Angus and Melanie? Here? Last night? Did she know him at all?

Stepping back in to the waiting room, she heard Angus still chatting to George in the surgery. What should she do? Confront him? He would think she was snooping.

Heart still pounding, her instinct was to leave. Quickly. Pack her things and go back to Sydney. She had made such a fool of herself. How could she trust him? But that was her usual response, flee if things get hard, or complicated.

Willing herself to calm down, she tried some self-talk. Take the emotion out of it. Be logical. Perhaps there was an explanation? Perhaps Melanie had gone in to tidy up. It made little sense, but she felt she owed it to herself to at least ask. Be an adult. Have a conversation. Angus, are you having an affair with Melanie? Angus did you rush in here last night to sleep with Melanie?

George came out of the surgery holding a wriggly Harry, Angus right behind them. "No problem George, I'll send the account at the end of the month."

Tipping his hat at Rose, George stepped out, with Angus locking the door behind him.

Turning, he looked at Rose and breathed out loudly.

"Thanks for your help, you arrived at the perfect time. Hungry?"

Rose searched his eyes. He looked tired. Like he had no sleep at all. "Yes," she murmured, looking down and fiddling with her handbag.

Angus didn't notice. He ushered her out through the back door in front of him, locking up and setting the alarm as he went.

They strolled to the coffee shop together, Angus speaking, a little too much she thought, about his busy morning and the patients he had tended.

They found a table at the back, away from the tourists who appeared to be getting ready to leave.

After ordering, Angus looked at Rose. "Is everything all right. You seem distracted?"

"All good. I spent the morning working the filly, she's coming along well." Rose thanked Cathy for the coffee as she set it down, returning with two ploughman's platters.

They ate in silence for a few minutes, then Rose leaned back and said. "So the alarm this morning. Was there no one there?"

Angus paused for a moment. "It was a false alarm, but I didn't want to come back and wake you again." He seemed a little uncomfortable and Rose had the distinct feeling he was omitting something.

"And Melanie? Is she unwell?" Taking another sip of coffee, Rose watched him through her lowered lashes. He hesitated and seemed to almost squirm. Definitely something to hide.

"Yes. Maybe." He seemed to search for the right words. "She has leave scheduled for the next two weeks and needed to go early."

"Really? Not much notice for you. On a clinic day, is it?" Rose watched his reaction.

"Oh. You know. Personal leave. Didn't like to pry." Then, grinning at Rose, he added "I had a great stand-in vet nurse!"

Wiping his mouth on the serviette, he picked up his coffee and downed the last of it. "Sorry Rose, but I need to get back to it, I've got large animal calls to make this afternoon." Standing up, he added quietly "See you at dinner? Can I bring something back for you?"

Stomach churning, Rose felt like throwing the rest of her coffee in his face and shouting "liar, liar!" Instead, she nodded at him. "No need, I'll whip something up."

He smiled and strode off.

Feeling confused and shocked, Rose sat mulling over the events of the past twenty-four hours. Something had definitely happened with Melanie. Angus was not telling the truth. What future was there if he wasn't honest with her?

Deep in thought, it startled Rose when Debbie sat beside her, a slice of orange and almond cake, with cream, on a plate with two forks.

"Dessert, girlfriend. I saw you with Angus. Tell all." Debbie pushed the plate and fork toward Rose, having already taken a bite herself.

"I really thought something was bubbling along there. That maybe Charlie knew what he was doing when he made his will. But it's not to be Deb. He's not the one for me." Angry tears glittered in Rose's eyes, and Debbie moved closer, letting her shoulder lean into Rose's in a show of solidarity.

"What is it Rose. Angus seems great. I've always thought he was one of the good ones. You know what I mean?"

"I think he has an arrangement with Melanie. Or something. I don't know. I felt so sure of him last night, but today, it's all blown away like a puff of smoke."

Debbie frowned. "Melanie? Really? I wouldn't think so, but ..." she chewed on her bottom lip.

"What is it Deb? Do you know something?" Rose pleaded.

"Not about Angus. Not really. But Greg brought some cattle in to the sale yards early this morning. He came in for coffee after. I'd just opened up. He said he saw Melanie driving out of town very early. He was concerned. He said her face was bruised."

"Bruised? Really? Badly enough he could see that when she drove by?" Frowning, Rose stared at the cake on her fork then placed it back on the plate pushing it toward Debbie, stomach churning. "Actually, I saw a bruise on her arm, looked like a handprint, when she was in here the other day. Maybe there's more to this."

She told Debbie about the alarm, Angus not returning. The unmade bed.

"I just don't know Rose. It doesn't ring true for me. Angus seems an unlikely domestic violence candidate." Debbie shook her head. "Melanie, however. She has hinted at romance with Angus, and they danced together at the party .... " trailing off, Debbie shook her head again.

"You need to ask him Rose. Just ask him if he is involved with Melanie."

"If he is, will he tell me the truth? If he is 'one of the good ones' would he have slept with me, while having an affair with Melanie? I sense he is hiding something. I'm not in so deep that I can't get out. Sure, I have feelings for him. Could even see a future for us. But let's face it, it's only been a couple of weeks." Speaking her thoughts aloud, Rose made a decision.

"I'm going home. Today. I'm due back at work in a few days, anyway. I can't involve myself with someone I can't trust. I need some space, for clarity. I want someone I can be sure of, like you are with Jamie." Smiling sadly, Rose nudged Debbie, slightly, with her shoulder.

"I understand Rose. Maybe some distance will provide perspective. As you say, you are due back at work, anyway. Will you come back every few weeks, check on the horses? Catch up with me?

"Of course!" Changing the subject, Rose mustered some enthusiasm to ask, "Debbie, do you have a dress design in mind? Are you having something made or do you need to go dress shopping? Do you think you could take a few days off to come to Sydney and we could hit the bridal shops together?"

"Yes! Bridal shops in Sydney, definitely! Perhaps in about eight weeks, if it suits you, I could take off for a few days. Lovely thought. I have some ideas, but I'd love your input," Debbie's excitement lit her lovely face up and Rose couldn't help but feel warmed by her friend's radiance.

"It's a date. I will call you next week. Right now, though, I need to speak to Douglas Barlow before I head off." Rose finished her coffee and stood up.

Debbie jumped up and gave her a huge bear hug and Rose turned away quickly, as tears pooled in her eyes.

Another hug and Rose marched up the stairs to Barlow's office. If Frances was surprised to see her, she didn't let on.

"Rose, dear, how are you? Douglas is free, if you wish to speak to him. I will bring tea."

Sitting before Douglas in his office, Rose calmed her breathing. She knew what she had to do.

"Douglas, I need to return to Sydney. To my job and my life

there. Please advise Angus Hamilton he can move into what was my parents' wing of the house. He can also use Charlie's study, as required. I would like him to care for my horses. I will employ a gardener, if you can recommend someone. I would also like a housekeeper or cleaner, just to do the inside of the main homestead once every three or four weeks.

"I plan to return every few weeks and for Debbie and Jamie's wedding. I will give adequate notice of any visit and ask that Angus not be in residence when I come." She sat back, looking at Douglas, who had taken notes while she was speaking.

"Further to this, I intend to offer the property to Angus when the three years are up. I don't believe I will ever live in this region again. There is nothing here for me."

Douglas put down his pen. "Has something happened Rose? Did you talk this through with Angus as you intended?"

"We talked. There is nothing more to add. Can I retain you, Douglas, to manage the gardener and housekeeper arrangements?" Rose stood.

Douglas came around the desk and shook her hand warmly. "Of course Rose. If you need to speak to me, or to Frances, we are here for you. I am coming to Sydney for a conference in a couple of months, may I meet you for coffee then?"

Rose smiled wanly at Douglas. Such a nice person. A caring person. She almost lost her composure, thought of telling him how close she had come to falling for Angus, had slept with him, then discovered his deceit about Melanie. The thought of saying this to Douglas brought a blush to her cheeks. The conversation would embarrass the dear man. Better to say nothing.

33

B emused at first, and then angry, Angus struggled to
understand exactly what Douglas Barlow was saying
on the phone.

"Rose has left? Today? Returned to Sydney?"

"Yes Angus. She asked me to advise you and make arrangements for you to move out to Barrington, into her parents' wing.
She said you had discussed this together."

"We had." Standing at the gate to Neale Campbell's yards,
waiting for them to bring in the stock, he was having trouble
understanding why Barlow was telling him this and why Rose
hadn't called him herself. Perhaps she had been called back to
work urgently?

"Call in to the office later, we're open until five, and we will
have the keys ready for you."

"OK. Thanks." Neale Campbell waved at Angus, indicating
they were ready for him to go to work. "I'll see you this afternoon Douglas, thank you."

Driving into town at the end of the day, Angus tried for the third time to call Rose on her mobile. No answer. He left a message, asking if she was OK. She did not respond.

By the time he reached Barrington and unlocked the house he was beginning to worry. He saw the note on the kitchen bench, propped against the kettle.

There is no easy way to say this Angus. I made a mistake and believe there is no future for me at the farm. My home is in Sydney. **Rose.**

Angus threw the note across the room, fury etched into his features. What the hell was she playing at? Leading me on? Sleeping with me just for fun? I wouldn't have thought it of her! Well, if that's the kind of woman she is, I'm better off.

Stomping to his end of the house, he opened the doors to let some air in. What changed her mind? He knew she had unresolved issues over her parents' deaths. Did she just need some time to process her history?

Shaking his head, he knew deep down that Rose was now a city girl. She had a career and a home in Sydney. She must have weighed up the pros and cons of a relationship and stopped it before it really developed, knowing she wouldn't return to the country permanently, and understanding that he wouldn't leave it.

Sighing, he went out to Charlie's chair on the veranda and took a deep breath. He had been so close to something special. He stayed there, looking out over the gardens and orchard, as the sun set.

34

Douglas Barlow was true to his word and sent Rose an email account of Angus' move to Barrington and the engagement of a gardener and house-keeper. He then emailed weekly, or rather, Frances emailed on his behalf, keeping Rose up to date with her accounts, often adding a short personal note at the end.

On one of these, the week after her return to Sydney, Frances mentioned Rosewood Beef had made a very high offer for Barrington. The offer was generous. They would take the land and subdivide to exclude the house, if she wished to retain it herself. Rose bit her lip while she read on. The group had purchased two more local properties.

How did she feel about that? Did she even want to keep Barrington? She doubted Angus Hamilton would offer the same price or that he would relinquish the house. She shook her head. This would be expressly against her grandfather's wishes and really, her anger at Angus had subsided. It was her own fault she had leapt in to bed with him so quickly, without understanding his values or romantic history.

Working back at her desk, editing a second book by the author of a scandalous first novel, poorly written in her opinion, Rose found it hard to concentrate. She had always loved her job, but lately she found herself re-writing more than editing. She was developing a desire to write seriously herself, tell a great Australian story, set in the country. A family saga perhaps.

Rose leant back in her chair. Why had she never considered this before? An Australian rural story with challenges and drama based on historical fact? Of course! She could use the story of her great great grandparents, when they settled the land and built the homestead, as a base for a gripping piece of fiction. Could she though? Was she good enough? She was an editor, not an author.

Her email beeped, and she saw it was from Debbie. Rose smiled. They had been having enormous fun sending links on potential wedding gowns to each other and they seemed to have settled on a style. Rose had found a very exclusive wedding boutique in inner Sydney that specialised in vintage original designer gowns and Debbie was coming next month for a first look.

However, when Rose opened the email, she saw it was not about the wedding at all.

Hey Rose, I just thought you may want to know that there have been rumours circulating that Angus Hamilton is working with Rosewood Beef. I did not believe it at first, but too many are referencing it. His practice has dropped off. The farmers, even Jamie and Greg are calling in Richards from Stroud instead, and his small animal clinic has dropped to once a week. I saw him go upstairs to Barlow this morning. *I thought you should know. If I hear more, I will let you know. Deb XX*

Damn! Really? It seemed unlikely. He had said he shared Charlie's view that the land should stay with the families who had farmed it for generations. Maybe it was true, though. She didn't really know him at all.

Spontaneously, Rose shot back a note to Debbie.

I'm coming down this weekend. I'll check in with Douglas Barlow and speak to Angus too. I'll arrive Friday, leave Monday. Perhaps we can have another girls' night? Saturday? Rose. XX

There. She will go down and check on everything. See if Freddie is OK with the horses. Catch up on Monday morning with Douglas Barlow, talk about the offer. Bring back a few of the papers documenting her family history and the early days on the farm. Perhaps she could outline a book, see if there was enough there to tell their story.

Still considering her visit, Rose whipped off an email to Frances Barlow, for Douglas.

Hi Frances, please let Douglas know I am coming out this weekend to check on the horses. I'll arrive on Friday afternoon and will leave Monday lunch time. Will Douglas have time to see me on Monday morning to discuss this offer? Also, please advise Angus that I will be at the homestead and I would prefer him to stay at the clinic while I am there. Thank you. Rose Gordon.

Later in the day she received a response from Frances, with an appointment to see Douglas at nine am on Monday. She had not spoken to Angus, as she understood his grandmother had passed away and he would be on the north coast to attend the funeral and visit his mother. Frances did not expect him back until Monday.

~

LEAVING WORK LATER THAN EXPECTED, it was almost dusk when Rose pulled up at the homestead. As she did, she saw movement down at the stables. Checking her watch, Rose stepped out of her jeep, stretched her legs for a moment, then walked to the stables.

Almost there, she saw it was Freddie, unsaddling Cotton in the yards. Waving, Rose smiled and said hi, leaning on the top rail of the yard.

"Hi Rose, I've just had the best ride on Cotton. She has a lovely nature, I really love her!" Freddie was glowing, her nose pink from the sun despite her wide-brimmed hat. The temperature had dropped now the sun was setting, but tendrils of hair curled damply around her face.

"Freddie. So pleased you are giving her some exercise. How are the others?"

"Yep. All good. Topper lets me brush him now, if I give him a handful of chaff and molasses first. And Stormy is gorgeous. I haven't done much with her, but she is lovely and quiet. I took Calico for a ride yesterday, just to give her some exercise too." Freddie had unsaddled the mare as she spoke and began brushing her down.

"It's getting late Freddie, how are you getting home?"

"Oh, sometimes Angus runs me home, I've been working at the clinic with him. It's been great there too. Otherwise Dad or one of the boys comes to get me about this time." As she spoke, a vehicle could be heard approaching. Its headlights on, Rose wasn't sure who it was.

"Did you know that Angus had to go up the coast a few days ago? His Gran died. I think he'll be back on Monday. I've got the keys to the clinic. I've been looking after the patients we have there. It's only two puppies and a cat, but Angus said I was up to it."

Rose could see the pride in Freddie's face and slightly more self-confidence than usual. Angus had made a good decision to give her work at the clinic, and she was happy to have Freddie looking after the horses too.

The vehicle had stopped; Rose could see Freddie's older brother Callum in the driver's seat. She walked over.

"Hey Callum, thanks for picking Freddie up. I was about to suggest I run her home tonight."

"Hey Rose. No problem. With Angus away we don't like Freddie being here by herself after dark. It's all good, she's going to come to footy training with me, then we'll go home together." Callum nodded at Freddie, climbing over the fence, a wide grin on her face.

"Come on Sis, or I'll be late for training."

Freddie ran around to get in the car, opened the door, then flew back to Rose, gave her a tight hug, before clambering in to the car.

Still waving to Rose as they drove out, a bit of Freddie's enthusiasm seemed to rub off and she chuckled to herself as she hustled back to the house.

Approaching the house, Rose could smell the garden before she could see it. The familiar fragrance of rose and lavender mingled as she walked up the steps, unlocking the door in the dark. She missed being greeted by Ruff.

Opening up and turning on lights in the main rooms, Rose looked about her in pleasure. The housekeeper had been, every surface shone. Walking into the kitchen, she opened the fridge. Ah. A bottle of Sauvignon Blanc stood in the door. She lifted it out and poured herself a generous glass. The 'Barrington homestead free pour' as Deb called it. Taking a sip, Rose strolled from room to room. Everything was tidy and in order.

Heading to the master bedroom, she saw the chest was still open, the albums and documents where she had left them on the floor. Sitting cross-legged on the large rug, wine beside her, she spent a happy couple of hours sorting through the documents, finding a treasure trove of family history in a large manila folder, tied with string.

Inside was a record of her great-great grandmother's arrival by ship, the original title deeds to the land, even architect drawings of the homestead. Holding the faded drawings up to the light, Rose squinted to see the name of the architect. Walter Liberty Vernon. Sounds impressive. She would look him up later.

Standing she stretched her legs and wandered back to the kitchen, planning to cook some eggs on toast for dinner. It was getting late. Opening the fridge, she pulled out the open bottle of wine and poured another generous serving. Deciding she couldn't be bothered with dinner, she wandered through the house again, wine in hand, looking more closely at its design. All the formal rooms and the master had very high pressed metal ceilings. The other rooms had tongue-and-groove timber ceilings and walls. The fireplaces were sandstone, the floorboards hardwood. It really is a beautiful old home.

Thinking about her lovely apartment in Kirribilli, Rose recognised she had elegant taste. The beautiful old two-bedroom apartment in Waruda Street was built in the 1920s, one of only six in the three level red brick block. All had beautiful views over the harbour to the Sydney Opera House.

Rose knew hers retained the original kitchen and bathroom, which needed renovating, but the rooms were large, high ceilinged and airy. If she sold the farm, she could renovate the apartment. If she sold the apartment she could hang on to the farm.

Still sipping her wine, Rose wandered all the way through the house to her parents' quarters. Not her parents', she told herself, for Angus lived there now.

The door was locked. Without giving it too much thought, Rose pulled her house keys from her pocket and tried one in the lock. Bingo. Opening the door, she told herself she would just have a quick peek, see what he had done with the place in the couple of weeks he had been there.

An old leather chesterfield couch took up much of the living area. It was large, but worked with the room. Rose remembered he had furniture at his mother's place. That was where he had gone for the funeral, so he would probably bring some of it back.

The tiny kitchen was tidy. She opened the fridge. Eggs, butter and a six-pack of beer. Going through to the bedroom, she saw the bed was made with navy covers and white sheets. Nice. He had a bit of style. She could see he needed the chest of drawers, he had an open suitcase sitting by the wall and a wicker wash basket full of folded tee's and jeans.

Peeking in to the bathroom, she saw navy towels and masculine items; shaving stick, razor, cologne. Finishing the wine in her glass, she turned slowly around. Angus wasn't here. Wouldn't be here until Monday. She could run a bath, soak in it, think about her Mum. Revisit those final conversations.

Putting the plug in, Rose started the water running. Going first to the main bathroom, she gathered up shampoo and conditioner, handmade soap bought from the markets, a bath bomb and bubble bath and her robe. Taking them back to the large bath she checked the water level, then padded back to the kitchen in the main house to pour another wine.

Picking up the bottle, Rose took the lid off, changed her mind and took the whole bottle and glass back to the bathroom, along with a small packet of Lindt chocolates she found in the pantry. Champion dinner she thought, beginning to feel a buzz from the wine she had consumed.

Dropping her clothes in the bedroom, she walked naked to the bathroom, humming a little as she went. The citrus scented candle perched on the chair beside the bath filled the room with a soft fragrance, complemented by the lemongrass bubble bath she had liberally tipped under the running tap while the bath was filling. Glorious bubbles covered the entire surface as Rose slid in to the water, hair in a messy bun on top of her head.

Reaching for her glass, she sipped again as she leant back, eyes closed. What had her mother talked about in those last few weeks?

35

It was after ten and Angus was beat. He had driven almost five hours from his mother's. The funeral was on Wednesday and they had spent Thursday sorting through Gran's things, his mother happy they had kept so many pieces of her parents' solid timber furniture in her garage.

Angus had been pleased to note the number of friends his Mum had in the area. The funeral was well attended and one neighbour, Barry, seemed more than friends. His mum didn't mention it directly, but something in the way they were together told him they were in a relationship. They were easy in each other's company. Relaxed.

Barry helped him load the furniture and Angus had liked the man for his humour and compassion, and no nonsense manner. If it was a thing, he was pleased. His mum had been on her own a long time and the last few years with Gran hadn't been easy. Dementia was an unpleasant disease, a loss of identity for the sufferer and heart achingly sad for family and friends. He admired his Mum's determination to care for Gran at home, but it had taken a toll, and he hoped she may live a little herself now. Perhaps Barry will be part of that. Angus decided that would be OK by him.

Glancing in his rear mirror, Angus checked the load in the back of his ute was secure. He had the chest of drawers and roll-top desk and a small breakfast table with two chairs. The extra weight had slowed him down and he had left just on dusk. His mother had asked him to stay, leave in the morning, but he was worried he had placed too much responsibility on young Freddie, taking care of the animals in the clinic over the weekend. He was keen to get home, get a good night's sleep, then get the furniture off early in the morning.

Pulling in to the homestead it surprised him to see Rose's Jeep. Why hadn't Barlow told him she was coming? Sighing, he remembered they weren't expecting him back until Monday, and he guessed Rose planned to be gone by then. The couple of weeks since he had seen her had him still questioning her reasons. Was it really because she could not see a future at the farm?

Hesitating a moment, he wondered if he should sleep at the clinic, but damn it, she didn't tell him she was coming and he needed to get the load off first thing in the morning. He was bone tired to boot.

Turning off the ignition, he walked quietly to the entrance of his quarters. Rose would most likely be asleep in her room in the main house. He could slip in, grab a few hours' sleep, get the furniture off early and be at the clinic before she woke. He could stay there the next couple of nights too, keep out of her way.

Still, he was curious. What would their reaction be if they saw each other? The attraction was strong, and he had almost imagined a future for them. Was it really so simple, that she didn't want to move to the farm? Could they discuss a compromise, perhaps? Time in the city and time at the farm. It was worth a conversation, at the least. It had surprised him when she left without speaking to him in person; for such a forthright woman it seemed out of character.

He unlocked the door and walked straight to the small laundry where he turned on the light and pulled off his boots and shirt. He wanted to just fall into bed, but he was grimy from handling the dusty old furniture, so he pulled off the rest of his clothes, shoving them in the laundry hamper.

Switching off the light he stepped back in to the living area where he detected a faint citrus smell, not unpleasant. Sweet.

Walking naked through the bedroom to the bathroom, the fragrance was stronger. With his hand on the door, he asked himself if he should open it. Was Rose taking a bath? In the dark? He didn't want to scare her, but the thought of her being this close made his heart race.

Tiredness forgotten, his senses heightened, he slowly opened the door.

The room was empty. He turned on the light. There was a candle in a glass jar, burned almost to nothing sitting on the vanity and traces of water on the floor. An empty wine bottle and glass were on a wooden stool at the foot of the bath.

Disappointed, Angus turned around once in the room. Rose had been here, taking a bath just as she said she might. If he had been half an hour earlier, he may have walked in on her. What would she have done? How would it be between them?

She could say she didn't want a life here, but there was *something* between them.

Showering quickly then brushing his teeth, Angus turned back the covers and climbed into bed. He would be up early, get the furniture off, then head to the clinic.

36

Stretching as she woke, the sun beginning to reach its warming fingers through the veranda window, Rose closed her eyes briefly and sighed. A whole bottle of wine last night, no wonder her temples were throbbing.

A noise from the rear of the house had her eyes open, her heart racing wildly for a moment. Was there someone in the house? The intruder? How could he know she had returned last night?

Creeping quietly from her bed, wearing a singlet and boxer shorts, she crept to her door. Cracking the door open, she could hear further noises coming from her parents, no, Angus' rooms. Picking up a riding crop from behind her door, she padded silently to the rear of the house. Peeking out, she saw the front door to the rear wing was ajar. Pausing, Rose contemplated the situation. It couldn't be the intruder, it sounded more like thieves. Maybe kids. Locals may know Angus was away for a few days and perhaps they hadn't noticed her jeep parked at the side of the homestead.

Just about to tiptoe away to call the police, Rose heard a man's voice, muttering quietly. Frowning, she took a deep breath, threw the door open fully and leapt into the room brandishing the riding crop like a sword wielding pirate, shouting "Stop right there, the police are on their way!"

Angus, startled, spun around, dropping the edge of the roll-top desk on his toe as he did.

"Fuck it!" Angus gently lifted the heavy desk from his foot, glancing at Rose, now with the riding crop lowered, backing toward the entrance.

"Um. Sorry! I thought there was a thief in here. You aren't supposed to be home." She waved the riding crop around for a moment.

Angus leant back against the desk, carefully removing his boot and sock. He looked up.

"And if there was a thief, what were you planning to do with that?"

"Hit him, you. Run. Call cops. Dunno really." Rose mumbled, feeling suddenly silly. A headache was kicking in and she squinted slightly, raising a hand to rub one temple.

"Why are you here? I thought you were away!" Rose felt her anger rising as Angus just stood there, grinning at her. Then she remembered *why* he was meant to be away. "Um, sorry for your loss ..."

Boot and sock in one hand, Angus took a step toward her. About to turn and flee, she saw his face screw up in pain. Instead she stepped toward him.

"Show me your foot? Is it broken?" Forgetting her own discomfort for a moment, she knelt on the floor to inspect it.

"It's OK. Little toe, probably just bruised." Embarrassed at her attention, he straightened up. "I came back early to make sure Freddie was OK at the clinic. She's been great, but it's a lot of responsibility for her." Nodding toward the desk, he added "I wanted to get this stuff unloaded, then head in to town. Couldn't leave it uncovered in the back of the ute."

"Hmmm. I'm no doctor, or vet, but it doesn't look broken, although the toenail is already turning black." Sitting back on her heels she looked Angus in the eyes for the first time. "Is there any more to unload?"

"No. This is the last piece." He began to put his sock back on.

Rose watched for a moment. She wished he wasn't here, but now that he is, and hurt because she startled him, the least she can do is be civil.

"It's early. Would you like breakfast? Scrambled eggs, coffee, toast? I need something myself, I've got a bloody headache." Remembering the full bottle of wine she had consumed the night before, she blushed.

Boot back on his foot, Angus took a tentative step toward her, limping slightly. "Well, considering my injury is because of you, I will take you up on that offer." He looked her in the eye, before adding "I'll get the coffee started while you ... get dressed."

Looking down at herself she blushed again, then looked him in the eye defiantly. "I can make breakfast in my pyjamas in my house if I want to!"

Grinning again he drawled, "and that will add another layer of enjoyment to my breakfast, thank you."

Damn it. He was a lying rogue, but she felt a physical jolt in her nether regions at his words. Turning on her heel she headed in to the main house, pausing at the door of her room as he limped behind her.

"I'll just ... throw something warmer on. Be right there." Closing her door in his face, she heard him laugh as he made his way down the hall to the kitchen.

Coffee aroma filled the kitchen when Rose appeared a few minutes later, sensibly dressed in jeans and tee. The breakfast table was set for two; a Barocca fizzing in a glass of water, headache tablets beside it at one setting.

Fresh chives lay on a small plate beside a carton of eggs, whisk and a glass bowl. Rose hesitated but hell, she really had a nasty headache. She popped two tablets from the packet and gulped them down with the Barocca. Glancing at Angus, she could see he was still grinning.

"Better?"

"Don't know what I was thinking last night. Drank a whole bottle of wine. Yes, thanks. This will help."

Busying herself with the eggs and chives, pouring in a dash of milk, Rose heated a pan and began stirring the egg mixture. Angus stepped around her and made two coffees', popping two pieces of bread in the toaster.

"How's your toe?"

"Will I get more attention if I tell you it bloody hurts?" Angus winked.

Turning her back to focus on the eggs, Rose tried to firm her resolve not to get close to him. Standing behind her, she could smell his clean-man scent as he reached over her head to extract two plates from the cupboard. He seemed to hesitate for a moment, before moving over to the table.

Bringing the pan to the table, Rose transferred the contents to the two plates while Angus lifted the toast out, putting a slice on each plate.

They ate in silence for a moment.

"Freddie is doing a great job with your horses, Rose. She rides Cotton most afternoons and has been tying Storm and Topper in the yard, giving them extra treats before brushing them down. She is a natural."

"Freddie was here yesterday when I arrived. Yes, I agree, she is good with the horses. Says she has loved working for you at the clinic too." Rose smiled recalling Freddie's animation when discussing the horses and the clinic.

"So, Melanie is back at work on Monday?" Needing to remind herself that Angus had been deceitful and had not acknowledged his relationship with Melanie brought a slight frown to her face.

Angus noticed, but looked down as he answered, pushing the last of his eggs on to his fork as he spoke.

"I haven't heard otherwise, so assume she will be back on Monday." He lay his knife and fork down, then stood, taking the empty plates to the sink.

"I'd better get in to the clinic, check on Freddie and our patients. Thanks for breakfast Rose, it is great to see you. I will, um, move in to the clinic for a couple of nights, as requested."

Hesitating, Rose thought for a moment. This arrangement is for three years. Is it really fair to make him leave every time she came home? They were adults. He has his own accommodation in a separate part of the house. Reaching a decision, Rose smiled briefly at Angus.

"It's OK. No need to sleep at the clinic. Stay here and get your furniture set up the way you want. We need not be in each other's way."

"Really? That's great Rose, thanks. I'll just wash these plates up ..."

Rose walked to the sink, nudging him aside, laughing. "Go. I'll do this. Penance for your sore toe."

Grinning broadly, Angus smiled down at her, then turned toward the hallway, exaggerating his limp as he half dragged one leg behind the other.

"Angus!"

He turned, looking hopefully at Rose.

"It was the other foot!" Laughing out loud, Rose turned back to the soapy sink. Feeling lighter than she had in two weeks, despite the headache, Rose felt she had made a mature decision.

37

S till smiling when he reached the clinic, Angus knew he
and Rose had taken a small step toward each other at
breakfast. The attraction was still strong, but she had
put up walls. Perhaps he could take them down, beginning this
weekend, brick by brick. For the first time in two weeks he felt
he and Rose may work out a way to move forward, together.
Crystallising this thought, he recognised how badly he wanted
to make it work.

Pleased to see Freddie there and the animals already fed
and watered, Angus wondered why he had been concerned. He
gave Freddie a ride out to Barrington to spend time with the
horses, leaving her at the stables with Rose while he sorted the
furniture out in his rooms.

Two hours later, dusty but happy with the results, he stood
back and looked around. The little table and chairs was the
perfect fit for the open living area and the roll-top desk filled
the small study. He would take some time to sand and polish it,

but in the meantime he could set his laptop up and put away
some of his personal papers. The large chest of drawers
provided a great solution for his bedroom and after a clean and
light polish he placed framed photos of his grandparents on
their wedding day and a lovely shot of his Mum and sister at his
university graduation on its top. Turning in a semi-circle in the
bedroom, with the doors open to his bathroom and the living
area, Angus realised it felt more like home than the flat at the
clinic ever had. It gave off an air of permanency, something that
had been missing in his life.

There was no opportunity to chat further with Rose, as she
had ridden around the farm with Freddie and then brought her
back for lunch. He would have liked to join them, but was
called to a local horse breeding property, where a mare was
having trouble foaling. He had wanted to ask Rose if she was
free for dinner, but felt uncomfortable with Freddie looking on.

Later that afternoon he met Rose in her car in the driveway,
going out as he was coming in. She waved through the windscreen, but it seemed she was heading out. Probably to see
Debbie and Jamie.

Not home when he turned in, Angus fell asleep hoping he
would have a chance to speak to Rose the next day.

38

After a late night with Debbie and Jamie, Rose struggled to wakefulness in the early dawn. She needed a drink of water. Greg had dropped in during dinner, but left after a quick hello, saying he had something to 'go to'.

"Someone, more like." Jamie had commented. "I think big brother is seeing someone, but it's a bloody secret at the moment. It must be serious as he isn't concentrating on working the farm, that's for sure."

Debbie had given Jamie a look, and he said no more about it, but Rose sensed tension between the brothers. Jamie left the girls chatting in the kitchen after dinner, heading to another room to watch the footy.

"How is it with Angus living there now Rose?" Debbie sat a plate of stuffed olives, homemade hummus, crackers and a selection of cheese on the table which they shared as they drank a small glass of red wine each.

"Not as bad as I thought. His rooms are separate. You know he came home late last night, wasn't expecting him until Monday, when I would be gone." Rose scooped dip on to a cracker, topped it with an olive and popped it into her mouth while Debbie leaned back and looked at her with narrowed eyes.

"Did you see him? Last night or this morning?"

"Uh huh." Rose continued to concentrate on her snack.

"And was it OK? Uncomfortable? Awkward?" Debbie leaned forward and removed the second cracker from Rose's hand, just before she put it in her mouth.

"It was OK." Rose knew she sounded defensive. "We're both adults. I, um startled him early this morning, unloading some furniture from his mother's. He dropped a chest on his foot. Sort of my fault, so I asked him to join me for breakfast. All good. Civilised. Told him he didn't have to stay at the clinic. You know, being grown up about it."

"Good. Sensible. So you're being grown up about it because you don't have feelings for him anymore?" Debbie looked smug as she loaded cheese on to a biscuit.

"Yes. No. Nothing really." Rose took a sip of wine, not meeting Debbie's gaze.

"Oh. Really? Nothing at all? Not even anger? Disappointment? Just nothing hey?" Debbie's tone was light, but Rose knew she was pushing for the truth.

Sighing, Rose pushed her glass away, picked up a napkin and wiped her fingertips slowly, before looking directly at Debbie.

"You want the truth, don't you?"

"If you can't tell me, who can you tell?" Debbie pushed her

own glass away, took a napkin and patted the edges of her mouth.

"There's something about him. He pulls me in. I fancy him like crazy and if he had jumped me at breakfast, I may not have pushed him away. But I have to be sensible. I can't trust him. I still don't know about the Melanie thing. Having him around may help me get used to him without, you know, feeling stuff..." she had begun strongly, but trailed off with the last few words.

"Stuff?"

"You know. Lust and stuff."

"And stuff? Girlfriend, I think you more than fancy him. I think you really, really like him. I think he could be the one, but it's complicated at the moment." Debbie reached across and covered Rose's hand with her own.

She continued quietly. "If your feelings are this strong, give him another chance. Talk to him about Melanie. Clear the air." Satisfied, Debbie leant back.

"You're right Deb. I should speak to him. Perhaps tomorrow."

Lying in bed, recalling the conversation, Rose wondered if the opportunity to speak frankly with Angus would arise today. Could she start the conversation, find some resolution, a pathway to move forward?

After a quick shower, Rose was dressed and in the kitchen, starting the coffee. No sign of Angus, he must have been called out.

～

THE MORNING FLEW by as Rose gathered together documents of

her family history. She had birth, marriage and death records, shipping manifests, two wills, the blueprints for the homestead and the original title deeds for the land and an ancient family bible with information recorded in the first few blank pages, faded and barely legible. In a nutshell, she had the basis of a story, a saga even, but the documents required more study and she needed to draw up a family tree to map the history. One idea was to write a memoir of sorts, in her great-great grandmother's 'voice' to tell the story of the early days. However, the amount of generational information unearthed had her wondering if it would be better told as fiction, based loosely on historical fact.

A rumbling in her tummy told her it was time for lunch. Standing, she stretched, then padded quietly to the kitchen. Still no sign of Angus. She was disappointed. Had hoped they would have an opportunity to speak.

Strolling to the stables, Rose noted the cool morning had turned into another warm, dry day. The atmosphere was dry. Dry air, dry earth. Long range weather forecasts could see no break in the drought, caused by a lengthy El Nino effect.

She messed around with Storm in the yards for an hour or more, hoping Angus would return, providing an opportunity to talk. Rose needed to understand his relationship with Melanie. Was it just work, or more personal?

Frustrated that Angus did not return, Rose saddled Calico and rode through the farm to the creek. Looking at the cattle in the homestead paddocks, there seemed less than there were two weeks ago. Had Angus sold some? Or moved them to a paddock further away?

A slight nudge of her heels and Calico stretched into an easy canter. Without forethought Rose turned toward the creek. The tree line came into view and she saw a temporary fence holding about twenty young Herefords along the creek flats where the grass was still green and nutritious. Good thinking. Perhaps Angus is rotating them in small groups to eat down the good feed in this spot. Definitely saves on buying in feed for the dry paddocks.

Not wishing to enter the fenced area and disturb the stock, Rose continued on to the boundary fence, where it had been cut three weeks before. Dismounting, she saw that it had been properly mended. It was a good job. Not just a vet, Angus knows farming. Sighing, she turned toward home. Irrationally deflated that there was still no sign of Angus, Rose unsaddled Calico, fed and watered her, then walked her back into the horse paddock. The rest of the mob looked healthy, raising their heads from the hay she had left earlier, to nicker at Calico. Topper trotted to Rose, pushing his nose into her hand. Leaning against his wither, Rose put her arm under his chin and rested her face against his.

Unbidden tears edged down her cheeks. Rose wallowed for a moment. Plenty of people have lost family, but how many have lost all their family? No living family. No lover. Friends, yes. But where is her place? What should she do? With her life, her career, the farm? Who can she ask for advice?

A few moments more and she straightened, wiped her tears on her sleeve, gave Topper a pat and dawdled back to the yards. Charlie knew she would be in this position. He used his will to give her options. As unexpected as the will was, it provided her with time to work out where her place was. To work out how to keep the farm, if she wanted to.

Her mother's words, in her last days, came back to her. "Sometimes we don't get what we think we want, but often it turns out to be exactly what we need. Keep your options open

Rose, don't make your path too narrow. Make it wide enough to share." Those words had a ring of truth about them now. Rose knew she could be stubborn and single minded. It had served her well in her career but had not helped her romantic life.

Back at the house, Rose thought about taking another bath, but worried it would send the wrong message to Angus if he came home while she was in his rooms.

Her phone beeped. A text from Angus.

Been out of town all day. Have you had dinner?

Smiling, Rose messaged back.

Not yet.

Pizza? I'm in town now, can bring some back.

Sure. Thanks.

OK. See you shortly.

Humming quietly, Rose set the table with plates, napkins and two wineglasses. Hearing the car, she opened the front door for Angus.

39

L
arge grin on his face, Angus held out two pizza boxes and a six-pack of beer.

"I'm starving. And thirsty. Beer first?"

Rose laughed, took the pizza boxes from him, setting them on the table before reaching for a beer. "You're a bad influence Angus Hamilton. You're the only person I drink beer with."

Taking a huge swig of beer, he said without thinking, "I'm pleased about that. I'd like to be the only person you do a lot of things with." He hadn't meant to say it out loud, but it was true. He had thought about this woman all day, hoping he would get back in time to share a meal with her. Time for a conversation ... and perhaps more than conversation. He registered the initial surprise on Rose's face as he said the words, followed by a light flush in her cheeks. He watched her sip the beer, eyes lowered slightly, knew she was thinking. Smart girl, always thinking. That's a good thing, but perhaps she lets it impede her feelings. Perhaps she overthinks.

Seizing the moment, he downed the rest of his beer, then reached over and took the drink from her hand before setting it on the table. Standing, Angus pulled Rose, unresisting, from her chair, wrapping his arms around her tightly. Bending down, he heard her soft intake of breath as he rubbed his stubbled cheek against hers, before growling in her ear, "I want you Rose. I want you now. Tomorrow. Next week. We can work this out."

Offering no resistance, Rose melted against him, sending hot lava through his veins. Moving his mouth over hers, he kissed her, long and deeply. She kissed him back. Urgently. Looking into her eyes, he moved his mouth against hers, more softly. She moaned quietly, allowing him into her mouth. Pizza forgotten, his hunger for her throbbed through his body.

Raising her head, Rose looked him the eye, drew a deep breath and moved slightly out of his embrace.

"One question Angus. I need to know if you are involved with Melanie. A relationship, sleeping with her, romantically attached in any way?"

"No. Not now, not ever."

He drew back and looked deeply into her eyes, then sighed. "Melanie has needed my help, protection even. I'm not sure who from. She won't tell. I've tried to help her. That's all I can tell you. It's all I know, in fact."

Rose seemed satisfied with that, he tightened his embrace. Walking backwards, his arms still around her, he took them into the living room and lowered her on to the rug while he kneeled over her, stripping off his shirt quickly. He unbuttoned her blouse and removed her bra, then kissed his way from her mouth to her breasts. She arched her back, and with one hand behind his head, pulled him closer. Working his way further down he rolled her linen pants down, kissing her naval, nibbling down to her underwear.

Lifting her bottom for him, he stripped off the last piece of clothing and sat back on his heels for a moment, just looking at her. Her face was flushed, her beautiful thick hair spread around her head and her chest rising and falling as she tried to control her breathing.

"You are beautiful Rose. So beautiful."

Her hands were working at the front of his jeans, struggling to get them undone. He stood and stripped them off, standing over her, naked, showing her how much he wanted her.

"So are you. Beautiful. Don't stop. Oh, Angus don't stop now."

Then he covered her body with his, kissing her deeply. Rocking her gently he found his way into her. Moist. Warm. Welcoming. He would love this girl now. Really love her. He would show her, make her understand that they could make this work.

40

Next morning at nine Rose bounded up the stairs to Barlow's office. She had considered dropping in for a coffee with Deb, but knew her face would give away she had spent the night making love with Angus. She wasn't ready for a Deb inquisition this early in the day.

Angus had been full of ideas about how Rose could split her time between the farm and Sydney. She had been caught up in the moment, had mentioned her plan to try some serious writing. Angus had seized the idea, telling her she could set herself up at the farm to write, perhaps work freelance as an editor for the publishing house, or other authors, as she worked on her book.

Angus had all but told her she was the one for him. There was no one else. Rose felt confident there was no one else.

Smiling at Frances as she strode through the door, Rose gave her a hug and made small talk about the weather for a moment.

"Douglas is free, Rose. Go on in, I'll bring some tea."

"Thank you."

Energised and somehow *lighter* than usual, Rose hugged Douglas before settling into a chair in front of his desk.

"You look well Rose. Blooming. It's lovely to see you smiling, with all that's happened in recent weeks."

As usual, his quiet, genuine demeanour gave Rose an extra shot of confidence.

"I understand an offer has been made on Barrington? With the option to subdivide the homestead from the farm?"

"Yes Rose. It came in last week. The group seems to be approaching owners more aggressively of late. They have offered a substantial sum and I have to advise that few other buyers would allow you to keep the homestead on a separate title. As your lawyer, I will tell you this offer is above market value." Douglas handed a two-page document to Rose. Her eyebrows raised when she registered the generosity of the offer.

"Having said that, Rose. I will add that your property is the key to the success of their project. Without the spring-fed creek on your land, the ability to access enough water, even in wet years, would be uncertain. Your property would provide long-term viability for the project. If you are interested in the offer, I would recommend that you counter offer. I believe the price could increase."

Brow creased, Rose re-read the letter of offer, then looked at Douglas. "And they are pressuring other locals to sell? Have any more accepted?"

"Well. I can't tell you that. The ones you already know, certainly. There may be others, but it is not public, so I cannot divulge these to you." Douglas paused while Frances brought in a tea tray, pouring it for them.

Spontaneously Rose said "Stay Frances. Join us. I'd like to hear your thoughts on this too."

"All right Rose. Thank you."

Rose read the letter again, saying nothing, while Frances fetched a third tea cup. When she returned, Rose asked, "And if I don't sell? If I make it clear that I will *never* sell Barrington? What happens to their project then?"

Frances looked at Douglas. Douglas spoke first. "As your lawyer, I need to advise you that this offer is already well above market value. In your lifetime you may never be offered this figure again."

Frances set her cup down and glanced at Douglas, before turning to Rose. "If you don't sell. If you make it clear you will not sell, now or in the future, we believe Rosewood Beef may move on to another area. We think it was your farm, and Charlie's age, that had them looking here to begin with. We also think someone local is working with them, has perhaps told them they can encourage you to sell."

Douglas added, "While they believe there is a chance you will sell, it is possible that fence cutting, dog killing and other types of harassment will continue. If you make it clear, there is no chance. Ever. These tactics may cease. Frankly, we have considered advising you *to sell*, if only for your own safety. However, Charlie would have hated you to give in to bullying tactics."

"What do you want Rose? For yourself?" Frances laid her hand on Rose's arm briefly.

"One more question before I answer that, if I may? If Rosewood gives up on this area, and moves to another, what happens to the farms they have already purchased, at top dollar, as I understand it?"

"Good question Rose. They would most likely be keen to sell those, and quickly. The properties would not value up to what they have paid, if they are not aggregating them into a large holding. They would have to take market value, and with the drought, that would be far less than they paid. They could hold on to them, of course, and wait for rain, which may improve the value slightly. But I believe they would cut their losses and try a different region."

"Thank you. I think I understand the situation now." Rose handed the letter back to Douglas. "Please respond, clearly, that the property is not for sale and will not be for sale in the future. Further offers will not be entertained."

A quick smile passed between Douglas and Frances. Douglas stood up and walked around his desk, to perch on the edge by Rose's chair. He took Rose's hands in his and took a breath. "You are Charlie's girl, through and through Rose. He would be proud of you right now. We are proud of you."

Frances nodded. "Can you manage Rose? Can you hang on to Barrington? Will the arrangement with Angus allow you to do that?"

"Yes. Yes I can Frances. If it gets tough, I will sell my apartment in Kirribilli. Barrington is in my blood. I will keep it."

BOUNDING BACK DOWN THE STAIRS, Rose looked in at the coffee shop. Debbie was at the coffee machine and gave her a wave to show she should take a seat. Rose looked at her watch. She needed to pack her bag and head back to Sydney.

On the verge of ordering a coffee to go, Rose saw Deb hand over to Cathy. She walked over to Rose, two take away coffee's in hand. Rose laughed and took one from her as they settled into seats at the edge of the shop.

"You look pleased with yourself." Debbie took a sip from her cup.

"I am. Rosewood Beef made another offer. A big offer. I've made a decision about my future." Rose saw surprise, then resignation, cross Debbie's face.

"Oh? What have you decided Rose?"

"I'm not selling. I'll sell the Kirribilli place if I have to. I'm hanging on to Barrington." Rose spoke firmly, then grinned at Debbie. "I'm hoping to spend more time here too. I will free-lance edit, if I can get the work. And research a book of my own. I'll look into renting my apartment out. It will take a few of months to sort it all out."

"I'm shocked. Really pleased, but shocked." Debbie had one hand to her mouth. "That is not what I expected you to say. Quite the opposite, actually. And when did you start referring to your apartment as 'the Kirribilli place'? It sounds like you have already decided to make a home here. Does this have anything to do with Angus?"

"In a way it does. But it's more to do with Charlie. The structure of his will gives me breathing space to hang on to Barrington. Gives me time to change my career path, slightly. I don't know if he hoped I'd make a match with Angus, and before you ask, yes, we are back on track." Rose raised her eyebrows and Debbie nodded.

"You've been at it again with him, haven't you? Wicked girl!" Debbie laughed out loud.

"Yes I have." Rose winked. "But Deb, even if it doesn't play out with Angus, I think I'd like to stay. It feels right. I have friends here. You and Jamie. The town has welcomed me home. I have deeper roots here than I realised."

Chatting for a few more minutes, Rose looked at her watch. "I really have to go Deb. I've got to get back to Sydney, but I should be down again in a couple of weeks. Before I rent the apartment out, perhaps you'd like to come down and have a weekend with me? Go bridal shopping?"

"Bridal shopping. Yes, please! Next month works for me."

A quick tight hug, another goodbye, and Rose left, only glancing back when she got to her car. Debbie was standing there still, smiling and waving. Rose took a deep breath as she got behind the wheel. It was a good decision. The right decision.

41

One of Rose's colleagues, Jeannie, popped into her office to mention they were getting Thai takeout for lunch, and would she like anything? The thought of Thai food, usually a favourite, made Rose feel queasy. Just the thought of it, actually. She smiled and shook her head and said she would pop out to get a roast beef sandwich from the café on the corner.

Jeannie smiled back, "you must really like that sandwich, you've had nothing else for lunch in the last two weeks."

Laughing, Rose waved her away before reaching for her purse. As she waited in line at the takeaway counter of the café, Rose's thoughts turned inward. Jeannie was right, she had been drawn to the same sandwich for a couple of weeks, since she had returned from Barrington. Some foods she usually enjoyed no longer appealed, and she had switched from strong coffee to herb tea for the same reason. Rose paid for her lunch and the petite citrus tart she had bought to have in the afternoon. The little tart had also become a daily favourite, but surely that was because she had tried Debbie's and it reminded her of her friend?

Back in her office, Rose nibbled on her sandwich and did some mental calculations. Her grandfather had passed away seven weeks ago. Rose had been back in Sydney for two weeks.

Oh hell, she thought, it was six weeks since she had slept with Angus the first time. Unprotected. She was on the pill, but they had not used a condom. Thinking back, she had missed taking the pill twice during those days, what with sitting up with old Topper all night in the stables and the drama with Ruff and the intruder, her schedule had been thrown out.

Rose squeezed her eyes closed for a moment, then emailed her boss saying she was feeling unwell and would work from home for the rest of the day and possibly tomorrow, as her friend was arriving in the afternoon.

Later that evening, the blue lines confirming her fears, Rose googled a "what to do when you have an unexpected pregnancy" forum. Reading through various comments on the site, she smiled at some and grimaced at others. Yes, her initial response was not to carry this baby, but lying in bed, her laptop open beside her, she hadn't cried when the test proved positive. In fact, the comments that made her smile the most were the ones that referenced their unplanned pregnancy as a blessing. Face it Rose Gordon, she said to herself, you're happy about this pregnancy. You just need to let Angus know. She nibbled her bottom lip. It was early days with Angus and they were a long way from making that sort of commitment. What if it didn't work out with him?

She should tell Angus. Explain she was making no demands; she was more than capable of raising a baby. Rose read a lot of manuscripts involving women with unexpected pregnancies. In romance novels it always worked out in the end. Rose wasn't so sure if it would in real life. The extra stress it would put on a new relationship could break it. Or make it. Angus has a strong sense of family, but she didn't want him to feel trapped.

They had spoken on the phone almost daily in the last two weeks, but were still very tentative about their relationship. Rose had not confirmed she was returning for good, had told Angus she was planning to take some time to work on her book, if her employer would provide freelance work. She hadn't put a timeline in place, had not worked up the courage to address it with her boss, having already had several weeks off. Only Debbie knew she wanted to make it permanent.

Next morning, while nibbling on vegemite toast, a favourite from childhood, Rose smiled to herself and patted her still-flat tummy. No real morning sickness and already six weeks along. The forum last night had a lot of comments from women with various health issues, including extreme morning sickness, swollen ankles, lack of concentration. Apart from a slight change in taste for certain foods, Rose had never felt better; her mind was clear, she felt strong and capable. Just like my great-great grandmother who travelled to Australia by ship in the late 1800s, pregnant and heading to a life in an unknown land, Rose thought. Yes, that's it. I'm a pioneer. Oh, I know women have babies every day, many of them on their own, but I feel like I can do anything. I will have this child. With or without Angus.

DEBBIE CAUGHT a taxi from the airport. After initial hugs and settling Debbie into the spare room, which doubled as a home office, they walked down the street for fish and chips. Eating in the park beside the harbour bridge, looking across at the Opera House and Circular Quay, they watched the ferries come and go and a large cruise ship head out to sea.

"Great fish and chips, Rose, nothing better in the world than freshly caught fish and hot chips. The only thing we forgot was a bottle of wine. A crisp Sauvignon Blanc would wash this lot down nicely," Debbie said while licking the salt from her fingertips.

"Sorry Deb, I was feeling a bit off yesterday and thought I'd wait another day before having a drink." Not exactly a lie, Rose thought, but she had not decided how to broach the subject with Debbie. She did not feel ready to answer questions about her pregnancy just yet. If she was going to tell Debbie it was Angus Hamilton's baby, shouldn't she tell Angus first?

"Something else on your mind Rose?"

"No. Not really. Have you heard any more about the Rosewood Beef? Have they left the area?"

Debbie was quiet for a moment. "Actually, it is a bit of a sore point at home. An offer has been made on Jamie's family farm. Jamie is dead against it and I thought Greg and their parents would be too. Their farm has been in the family almost as long as yours, Rose," Debbie sighed.

"The offer, however, is enormous. I can't understand why, to be honest. Without your place it makes little sense. I wanted to talk to you about this in person too, rather than over the phone."

"Talk to me?" Rose asked. "Why?"

Debbie looked confused. "I know you said you wouldn't sell, but there is a rumour that you have accepted an offer on

Barrington. As the Tait farm is on your boundary, it is worth more if they can get both. Jamie and I were a little surprised, even hurt Rose, that you didn't tell us you changed your mind. We understand. It is an offer that will never be repeated."

"That's not true Deb! Not a bloody word of it! Fuck! Who is doing this? Yes, an offer was made. No, I haven't accepted. I've told Douglas Barlow to refuse and that no further offers will be entertained!" Rose stood up, pacing back and forth as she spoke.

"Really?" Debbie looked hopeful. "Greg was so sure...?"

"Greg? What's Greg got to do with it?"

"I don't know Rose. He said he spoke to you..."

Rose was angry now. She knelt in the grass in front of Debbie and held her shoulders. "Why would he do this? He is Jamie's brother and I have all the respect in the world for Jamie, you and his parents. But Greg. I'm not sure I trust him. He can be so nice, but when you catch him with his guard down, I don't know. He is selfish. He always was, and footy stardom made him worse."

Debbie grimaced. "To be honest, Jamie is not loving having Greg home on the farm. In the beginning he thought it would be great, he looked up to him so much when they were young. But Greg takes advantage of their parents, he doesn't take much interest in the farm and lets Jamie handle the work. Jamie had thought after we get married, we could offer to buy Greg out. Greg goes out drinking most nights. We think he is seeing someone, but he doesn't say who. At one stage we even thought it might be you Rose, before you came home last time.

"What the fuck is he up to? I need to tell Jamie." Debbie reached for her phone but Rose put her hand out and said quietly, "Wait, there's more. I should tell you now, it will be obvious soon enough."

Rose took a deep breath, and couldn't help a small smile as she added "I'm pregnant. I only found out yesterday. To Angus."

Debbie looked stunned for a moment, then threw her head back and laughed. "Rose Gordon. I can see you're not upset so I am assuming you are going to be a Mummy. My gosh girl, you don't do things by halves!"

Rose laughed too, finally able to admit out loud that she was happy about this baby. "You can't tell anyone Deb. Not even Jamie. I have to tell Angus first. I don't want him to think I want anything from him, but he needs to know."

"Why?" Debbie asked.

"Why what?"

"Why don't you want anything from him? You didn't accidentally have sex. It was intentional. I know you Rose. I know you care for him. Why rule out a proper relationship, marriage even, before you speak to him?"

"Because we have only just started to get to know each other. Because he is exactly the sort of man I've always wanted and he has the power to hurt me!"

"Well that's true. The only people that can really hurt you, are the ones you love. I think you love Angus." Debbie smiled sweetly at Rose.

"Maybe I do. Or maybe I could. But I don't want him to be with me for the wrong reasons. It's more complicated than ever!"

Back in Rose's apartment, the girls made hot chocolate and chatted until the early hours. They focused on bridal shopping for the next two days. Rose would come back to Barrington to speak to Angus. And she needed to contact Douglas Barlow to see if he could put a stop to rumours she had sold the farm.

A brisk walk along the harbour to a little café for breakfast kick-started their day. Debbie laughed that they would not have been up so early and feeling great if they had spent the night drinking wine, like usual. Rose said she wasn't missing it at all and apart from her taste buds changing somewhat, she was energised and enthusiastic.

The weekend passed quickly and after trying on eight vintage designer originals, Debbie had her wedding dress, shoes and veil. The bridal shop would make something to work with it for Rose to wear.

Rose drove Debbie to the airport. They had discussed Greg, and Debbie said Jamie needed to know that he was lying about an ongoing friendship with Rose. She also wanted Jamie to know that Rose had not signed a contract to sell to the feedlot and wasn't planning to. Debbie promised not to mention the pregnancy until after Rose had spoken to Angus.

ONE WEEK LATER, Douglas Barlow was due in Sydney and Rose still hadn't spoken to Angus. Nervous about his reaction, she told herself she should do it in person, but hadn't found time to make the trip home. She thought she would have dinner with Douglas and catch up on the news first.

Debbie emailed or messaged most days and Rose knew that the Tait family was undergoing its own internal discussions, as Jamie had clarified that he and Greg could not work the farm together.

When Greg blustered that he would marry Rose and work

her property, Jamie told him firmly, in front of their parents, that he knew there wasn't a relationship with Rose and never had been. Greg had moved back to Sydney 'temporarily' to follow up a business opportunity there, and it relieved Debbie and Jamie. Jamie wanted to maintain a relationship with his brother, but not at the cost of the farm and his integrity.

Rose and Douglas met for dinner at a seafood restaurant in Darling Harbour. Douglas said several times that he should have brought Frances, she would love the restaurant. Rose felt her heart glow hearing Douglas speak about Frances so warmly after almost forty years of marriage. Small talk aside, Rose asked how the farm was.

"It's never looked better, Rose. Angus had a downturn in his practice and he has spent more time on the farm, repairing fences, planting pasture. He sold off some of his stock, which gave him some breathing space financially, and since the Tait family put the word out that they are using Angus again for their large animal work, business seems to have picked up a little. Rosewood Beef have gone quiet since you refused their offer Rose, and I heard that they are buying up in Armidale region now.

"I told Angus I was seeing you and he sent his regards and asked me to tell you that old Topper and the mares are well. The gardener is doing a wonderful job on the roses, although I suspect Angus spends some time on those too."

Rose was surprised, picturing Angus working in the garden, caring for her roses brought tears to her eyes. Damn pregnancy hormones!

Douglas said her name twice before she registered it. "I'm sorry Douglas, what were you saying? I was thinking about the old stallion just then."

Douglas smiled. "It may not be appropriate for an old man to remark on, but as I have known you all your life, I don't think you would mind me saying that you have never looked lovelier Rose. You are a picture of health, that's for sure. Perhaps the sea air here in this beautiful harbour city suits you.

"Having said that, do you think you might make a trip home soon? Check in on the farm and the house and your animals, catch up with old friends and perhaps find time for a meal with Frances and myself?"

Rose put her hand over Douglas's and said, "I don't mind at all. A compliment from a dear friend such as you is a compliment indeed. And yes, I do feel particularly well. I am planning to drive up next week. The sea air suits me, but I think the country air even more so."

DRIVING to Barrington the following week, Rose thought through all that had occurred in the last couple of months; the death of her grandfather and his unusual will, the forthcoming wedding of Debbie and Jamie, the beginning of something with Angus and the permanent outcome. Rose patted her tummy and smiled happily.

Her pregnancy was proving to be remarkably uncomplicated. She had been an only child and without her grandparents and her friendship with Debbie, would have been very lonely. She had always wished for a big noisy family, but it was possible she would raise this one on her own. She wasn't at all keen to railroad Angus into a permanent relationship.

Since discovering her pregnancy Rose felt uncomfortable speaking to Angus on the phone. She was convinced she needed to tell him in person about the baby. That was the only way she could judge his reaction. Sexy phone conversations seemed inappropriate, given the circumstances, and she could sense his frustration at the slight cooling in her tone when he called.

Less than an hour away, Rose called Debbie's mobile number and left a message that she would come to the café for a bite to eat before heading out to the farm.

Rose walked into the café and wondered if it was obvious she was pregnant. Her tummy was still flat, but she felt so different. Softer. Stronger. Strange feelings. She beamed when she saw Debbie rush toward her and pull her to the far end of a long table.

"Does Angus know you're coming Rose? Have you spoken to him at all?"

Rose smiled. "No. You know I want to see his reaction when I tell him. I don't want him to feel trapped by my news."

Debbie groaned. "Rose. Wait until I finish here. I will come with you. I don't want you going out there by yourself."

Debbie's concern started to crumble Rose's resolve. "Why Deb? What's going on? I don't need you with me for this, but bless you that you would do it."

"Angus is not alone at the farm. Melanie is there. She's been there since yesterday, with her daughter."

Astounded, Rose felt a sharp pain in her chest. She paled, then remembered Angus telling her that Melanie was dealing with problems and he would protect her. She was sure this was it. Rose needed to put her own feelings toward Melanie aside and help Angus support her. It might not be the best moment to tell Angus about the baby. She would judge that when she got there.

Reaching out, Debbie took her hand. "I'm so sorry Rose. I had hoped …. Well, it doesn't matter now. I didn't want you turning up out there without warning. That's why I want to come with you."

Her cheeks flushed, Rose reached for the glass of water Debbie had put in front of her and downed it quickly. "It's fine Deb. Angus is not romantically involved with Melanie. I understand that he has helped her previously … with personal stuff."

Ignoring Debbie's surprise, Rose gave her a quick hug and left. She didn't notice Angus pull in to the café as her own vehicle pulled out.

42

R   ose. That's Rose's car. Heading to Barrington, most
       likely. He glanced back at the café. Debbie was
       standing near the footpath. He raised his hand,
and she nodded and walked inside.

Melanie. They know Melanie and Tiffany are out at the
homestead. Shit. Small towns. Bloody hotbeds of gossip. He
didn't want her there, but what could he do when she came to
work yesterday, bruises on her arms and god knows where else.
Refusing to go to the police. Too scared. Whoever is doing this
is threatening her, and Tiffany.

He thought it was her ex-partner in the beginning, but no
longer. It seems she has become attached to some sort of mob-
ster, hinting he is involved in dubious business dealings. Angus
told her he couldn't help, to go to the police. But she cried, said
Tiffany was at risk. That he wouldn't harm them if they stayed
at the farm for a few days. He'd give up and leave town. She'd
be done with him, she said.

He raised his eyebrows. Would Rose be upset to learn Melanie was at the farm. He had told her, as much as he could, that Melanie was dealing with a difficult situation. Rose's attitude, since she had returned to Sydney three weeks ago, had changed dramatically. He was beginning to think she was moody, or flighty. He believed they had made a tentative agreement to give it a go. She had even talked about spending more time at the farm. Confused, Angus opened the door of his vehicle.

He had been planning to go to Sydney for a few days, try to see her. Talk to her on her home turf. Show he was willing to consider a flexible arrangement. See if there were genuine feelings between them.

He just needed to see Melanie and Tiffany safe. He'd never forgive himself if something happened to either of them.

43

Pulling in at the homestead, Rose sat for a moment. Melanie's Toyota Corolla was parked to one side but there was no sign of Angus's ute. Taking a deep breath, Rose wondered if Melanie and Tiffany were staying in Angus' part of the house, or whether he had given them the spare room in the homestead.

Steeling herself, Rose let herself in through the front door. Not wanting to startle Melanie, she called out.

"Hello. Anyone home?"

Walking in with her bag, all was quiet.

Placing her bag in her room, she opened the door to the spare room. Clothes were strewn across the bed and a child's teddy was propped up on one pillow. Closing the door again, a sudden movement behind her startled Rose.

Spinning around, she was face to face with Melanie. Neither spoke for a moment.

Melanie raised her chin, glaring at Rose. "You can't throw me out. Angus said I can be here!" Fear and defiance gave impetus to her words.

Stepping back slightly, Rose, determined to maintain her composure, spoke quietly but firmly. "It's OK Melanie. You can be here. You and your little girl."

Surprised, Melanie seemed to lose momentum. "Um, Ok. Thanks. Angus is out on calls…"

"Is Tiffany at school?" Rose thought the woman might relax if she showed an interest in her child.

Somewhat nervously, Melanie responded. "Tiffany is due on the school bus later. I was just using the laundry, getting some wash done …"

"Ok. I will head down to see the horses. I'll see you later."

Pleased with herself for her civility, Rose strolled down to the yards and watched the horses feeding for a short while. Freddie would be here after school. Perhaps she would go for a gentle ride with her. Her grandmother had often told how she rode well in to the seventh month of pregnancy, so Rose felt sure there was no reason she shouldn't ride too.

It was too early for Freddie and Rose suddenly realised how wound up she was, and tired. Perhaps a short nap first. Walking in to the house, all was quiet again. There was a faint hum coming from the laundry, it sounded like Melanie still had the machine going.

Halfway down the hall, Melanie popped out of her room in active wear. An attractive woman, she looked fit enough to run a marathon. Actually, Rose thought as she approached, she looked not so much fit, as thin. Really thin.

Melanie gasped and went to step back inside the room, but Rose was too quick. "Melanie. Wait. Are you all right?"

Rose frowned as Melanie hesitated. Not only was she thin, but she had a lot of bruising on her upper arms. Old bruising and new.

"I'm fine Rose. Going to do yoga out on the lawn. It keeps me in shape." The last words were said with a hint of pride, but Rose sensed an underlying sadness. And something else. Fear? Nervousness?

"Melanie. You look great, I can see that. But these bruises? They look painful." Rose reached out and tentatively touched the other woman's arm. Melanie winced and drew back.

"I'm fine. Clumsy. You know, messing around with Tiffany, sometimes it gets rough." She began to walk away.

"Really? Is that the truth?" Rose went on. "Who did this to you Melanie?"

Melanie stopped, her back to Rose. "No one. Just clumsy, as I said."

She turned to face Rose, her face screwed up in anger. "What do you care anyway, you never liked me."

Rose hesitated, but said calmly. "We may not have been friends Melanie, all these years. But we are both women. And we both know that anyone who hurts a woman in this way is not a good person. This should be reported to the police."

Rose looked directly in to Melanie's eyes. "Are you safe here? Is Tiffany safe? I can help you Melanie. You're don't have to deal with this alone." Rose said it and meant it.

Brushing away a tear, Melanie's face crumpled. "I'm not alone. Angus is helping. I'm staying here for protection. It's not safe for Tiffany and me at home."

"Oh Melanie." Rose stepped forward and wrapped her arms around the other woman briefly. She led Melanie to the kitchen and sat her at the table, while she busied herself making tea.

"Does Angus know who he is protecting you from? Do the police know?"

Melanie's reaction was instant. Crying and yelling she stood, her hands balled into fists at her side, shaking. "No! He doesn't! No one does. I'll never tell. He will hurt Tiffany. It's ok if he hurts me, as long as Tiffany is safe!"

She's bloody terrified. Whoever is doing this has her absolutely terrified. No wonder Angus has her staying. Hell. I wonder what we are dealing with. Who we are dealing with. And I hope he doesn't know where she is right now! Rose sat down and pushed a tea cup across to Melanie. For a moment Rose thought she would walk away, but she sat down and took a sip, before roughly brushing the tears from her cheeks.

Mumbling, Melanie said 'Thanks Rose. I appreciate your concern, I really do. You caught me unawares." She inhaled sharply. "I've kept Tiffany safe all this time. If I stay here for a few days, I think he will give up. It has to end. I'm sure it will end."

Shivers ran across the back of Rose's neck at her words. It sounded ominous. "I hope you're right Melanie. I'm here for two days if you want to talk. Or if you need anything. Really."

"Thanks for the tea." Melanie stood. "It's almost time for the school bus. Freddie will be on it, she'll walk with Tiff to the house. Yesterday she took her down to see the horses, let her help with the feeding. She really loved it." Melanie smiled at Rose and for the first time, Rose glimpsed the woman she really was. Scared as Melanie was, she was doing all she could to keep her daughter safe. Rose knew, instinctively, that she would protect her own child with the same passion. A connection, of sorts, had been made.

"All right. Let's all go down to the horses when the girls get here. I'll make some afternoon tea. They'll want a cool drink and a snack first."

Tiffany was shy with Rose, but once they were with the horses she chattered away, asking dozens of questions. Rose answered some, but was happy to let Freddie hold the little girl's hand to show her how to pat the horses, and feed them apples from her hand. She smiled at Melanie, who flushed with pleasure and smiled back.

They decided not to ride and Freddie was picked up by Callum shortly after. Walking back to the house, Melanie's mobile rang. She glanced nervously at Rose, then looked at Tiffany.

Rose took the little girl's hand. "Come in and tell me what you did at school today. Do you have any homework?" She left Melanie to take her call. As she walked into the house, she heard Melanie whisper, "No. Let it go. Let it end. Please let it end."

Good. She sounded firm. Perhaps it was all ending. Although the bastard, whoever he is, should be charged for what he has done to her, but perhaps it's less confronting if he just leaves.

Melanie took Tiffany for a bath, Angus was still not home when she returned with the little girl, damp hair in pigtails and wearing pink pyjamas.

"Angus messaged to say he would be late; he is all the way over at Scone at Bell Trees horse stud." Melanie looked concerned for a moment. "Rose, I told him you are here. He said he already knew."

"It's OK Melanie. I need to chat about a few things with him, but they can wait until tomorrow." Standing at the kitchen bench, an array of ingredients in front of her, she added "I will rustle up some home-made pizza. I have enough for all of us, if you and Tiffany would like to join me?"

"Yes. Yes please Rose." Tiffany was bouncing up and down on her toes, smiling at Rose. "Please Mum, can we have pizza with Rose? She said she would tell me all about Topper and the other horses. Please?"

Melanie laughed. She gently rustled her daughter's head. "Sure Tiff, if Rose says it's ok." Looking over the child's head, Melanie smiled at Rose. "Thank you Rose. It was going to be toasted sandwiches. Angus asked me not to leave the farm today, and his kitchen is a bit bare."

Tiffany helped Rose make the pizzas while Melanie set the table. The women focussed on the little girl and Rose could see how she opened up, forgot her shyness, in the safety of their company. She marvelled again that Melanie had raised her alone and kept her safe, despite her own ongoing trauma. How little she had known about this woman.

Debbie sent a text to Rose in the early evening.

Are you ok? Everything OK out there with Melanie. Worried about you. x

All good with Melanie and Tiffany. Angus not home yet, I'll chat with him in the morning..

Good for you. Come for coffee tomorrow.

I will. Thanks.

Feeling pleased with herself, Rose washed up while Melanie put Tiffany to bed and read her a story. Half an hour later Melanie came out, said she was tired too. She thanked Rose for dinner and her support. Added she had some thinking to do. Rose understood that to mean perhaps Melanie would go to the police and report the abuse. Feeling satisfied, and more than a little tired, Rose turned in. Angus was still not back, but perhaps he had stayed the night at Bell Trees. It was quite a drive over the Barrington Tops and fraught with hazards at night. Mobs of kangaroos would be on the move, the drought spurring their constant need to find feed.

44

A noise outside her bedroom jolted Rose awake. She looked at her phone. Almost midnight. Most likely Melanie using the bathroom down the hall, or even Angus returned. Listening for a few moments, the house seemed quiet again and Rose rolled over, her back to the bedroom door.

She woke again, thought she heard someone whisper "No!" Louder this time. "No!" It was Melanie, and sounded like she was just outside her door. Rose moved quickly, the blankets thrown back, her legs already out of bed when her door banged open. Rose screamed. It was dark but she could make out the shape of a large man in the doorway. Something covered his face. A balaclava? Melanie was pulling on his arm, trying to drag him back.

"Come away. Don't do it! Just leave! Don't wake Tiffany, please don't wake Tiffany!" Her words were urgent, but quietly said. Rose could sense she was crying, but couldn't see her clearly enough to be sure.

The man growled with an animal intensity and threw Melanie off. She hit the wall in the hallway and slid to the floor, now silent.

Heart rate rising, Rose raced to the door out to the veranda. There were top and bottom locks and he was on her before she had them free. He stank of beer, and spirits, and pulled her back from the door, almost wrenching her arm from its socket. Pain flashed through her shoulder.

Rose screamed and hit out, but he growled again and shoved her roughly on to the bed, falling on top of her. Holding her arms above her head, he tore her tee shirt from neck to hem, exposing her breasts. Rose tried to kick out, but he had her legs pinned between his. He was bigger, stronger, drunk and aggressive. There was something familiar about him, but she was fighting for her life and couldn't pinpoint what it was, or who it was.

He sucked at one breast, before biting it sharply, drawing blood. Rose cried out and increased her attempts to dislodge him. He moved off her enough to rip her boxer shorts down. Rose thrashed from side to side, making it difficult for him to focus. He removed one hand long enough to punch her in the side of the head. Hard.

Blinking rapidly, Rose tried to remain conscious, but could feel herself disappearing into the bed, the mattress seeming to envelop her. He was on top of her again, using his knees to spread her legs. She tried to clamp them closed, but they had turned to jelly.

A moment of clarity. She thought of her unborn baby and Melanie's resilience and bravery. Rose wriggled and rolled, moving as much as she could to prevent him entering her. He had a tight grip on her wrists, holding her hands over her head with one massive hand. His other was now across her mouth and nose. Struggling for breath, she tried to summon the strength to dislodge him.

From the corner of her eye she saw another shape enter the room. Small. Melanie? Something in her hand glistened in the sliver of moonlight creeping through the shutters.

Melanie pounced, shoved the thing into his side. Once. Twice. He roared. "Fucking bitch!" at the same moment lifting himself from Rose, on to his knees, taking his hand from her nose and mouth to backhand Melanie across the jaw. Her light body flew across the room, crumpled in the doorway. Rose brought her knee up, hard, between his legs and he turned back to her.

"I'll kill you for that, slut!" he slurred, but his movements seemed slower. Taking a chance, Rose slid from under him and limped to the doorway. Not sure if Melanie was breathing, she pulled her from the room and slammed the door, dragging a hall table in front of it. Adrenalin pumping, she raced out to the veranda through the back door, covered in the remnants of her tee shirt, hastily shoved a wicker outdoor chair under the door handle, locking the intruder inside.

That's when she saw it. The ute. The ute that Angus drove. Parked just beyond the house. Angus! It is bloody Angus! The bastard. The lying fucking bastard. Crying, she ran inside. Reaching the phone in the hallway, Rose dialled triple zero, covering herself with a throw rug from the back of the sofa as she stood shivering, waiting for an answer.

Triple Zero. What is your emergency?

Intruder. Rapist. I need an ambulance and police. Barrington Homestead.

Is he still in the house?

Yes. Locked in a room. He's hurt. My friend is unconscious. There is a child too, unhurt.

Police and ambulance on their way.

Rose hung up and ran to Melanie. There was no sound coming from her own room. The bastard! Disbelief mixed with horror. Rose touched her stomach, then vomited in the hallway. Angus! Bloody Angus! Did he kill Charlie too? And Ruff? What hold did he have over Melanie?

Turning the light on in the hallway, she knelt beside Melanie. She was breathing shallowly, but unconscious. Opening the door to the spare room, she saw Tiffany sitting up in bed, crying into her hands soundlessly. Fuck! What has the child heard?

Seeing her mother on the floor, Tiffany leapt from the bed and ran to her. Kneeling beside her she patted her face. "Mummy, mummy," she whispered. Rose put her arms around Tiffany, listening for movement from the room she had barricaded.

Moments later the sound of distant sirens, getting louder, could be heard. The police, just a few minutes away. A crash and a roar came from her bedroom. Rose stood, quickly pushed Tiffany back into the spare room and was dragging Melanie in after her when the back door at the end of the hall slammed open from the outside.

A large figure was silhouetted in the doorway. Another one? Two of them? Who? Rose kept dragging Melanie as the figure stalked closer, striding into the lit hallway.

"Rose! Rose. Oh my god are you all right? Melanie? Tiff! Angus stood before her. Rose looked at him, confused, as the door to her bedroom was shoved open, knocking the hall table over. The bastard began climbing out over furniture, bleeding and groaning. The sirens were close now; Rose had unlocked the front door.

Angus strode to the groaning man, grabbed him by the shirtfront and slammed him hard in the jaw. Twice. Leaving him on the floor, unmoving. Angus looked at Rose in horror. He saw the man's pants were undone. Saw the blanket covering her body and the torn tee shirt. Two steps and he had her in his arms. "Rose. Oh Rose. What has he done to you?"

Police filled the hallway, then paramedics. Rose was shivering, shock setting in. "Take Melanie first, please take Melanie first." She put her arms around Tiffany, holding her tightly as Melanie was lifted gently on to a stretcher. Her temples began to pound as she saw the police standing over the intruder. His side was covered in blood. Melanie had stabbed him, had tried to stop him, bless her. As the balaclava was pulled from his head, she drew in a breath, looked at Angus in shock. Greg Tait. Greg bloody Tait.

45

D eb hadn't wanted a traditional hen's party, rather something more refined, in keeping with the dress she had chosen and the understated elegance of the wedding and reception. The high tea suited Rose perfectly, as she had chosen not to drink during pregnancy. She wore a swing jacket over wide leg pants, and as her bump was small, she thought most people would just assume she had gained a little weight.

Frances Barlow looked at her a couple of times, smiling, and as Rose was leaving the bathroom and Frances was waiting outside, she started to say something. At that moment, they were called back to the party for the opening of presents and the moment was lost.

While she did not want to lie, she wasn't sure what she would say about her pregnancy. Angus had agreed they should say little until it was obvious. The whole town was still buzzing with the news of Greg Tait's arrest, his assault on the women at

Barrington. It wouldn't be obvious at the wedding ceremony she was wearing a very elegant coat over a matching dress in pale mint, in keeping with the late 1950s style of Debbie's tea length gown.

Rose knew she looked well in her outfit and was feeling radiant as she walked down the aisle. Seeing the look on Jamie's face as he watched his bride walk toward him, stunning in her vintage gown, was priceless. So much love. Debbie was a lucky girl. Angus stood at Jamie's side in place of his disgraced brother. They had become closer, all of them, in the last few months.

The reception was literally in full swing. In keeping with Debbie's theme, they had a six piece swing band, with the guests enjoying the departure from the usual rock-and-roll or country music played at local weddings. Definitely classy, Rose thought. She had been sitting at the bridal table beside Debbie, with Angus on the other side of Jamie. Debbie's parents were along-side her and Rose had enjoyed the conversation; chatting about local issues, federal politics, travel, books and music. Rose had no idea they had travelled so extensively in recent years and were very well read too. Debbie's mum declared no one was writing Australian stories anymore. Rose smiled to herself at that. She considered the outline of her own work in progress and thought Debbie's mother would be a great beta-reader for it.

The bridal waltz began and Jamie escorted Debbie on to the dance floor. She looked beautiful, and he was handsome and sophisticated in his tuxedo. After a few moments the parents of the bride and groom took to the floor and Angus held out his hand to Rose. She hesitated for a moment, then removed the coat from her gown, her bump now visible and stood up to move to the dance floor. Rose held her head high as they began to dance, but could hear murmurings from the crowd. Let them talk, Rose thought. I have nothing to be ashamed of. The band was playing a two-step and Rose was surprised, and delighted, that Angus had the moves. They laughed together as they sailed around the dance floor.

They smiled to see little Tiffany dancing with her grandfather, Ross Tait, her tiny feet standing on his toes as he moved her around the dance floor in a slow waltz. Moving back to their table, Angus and Rose sat with Melanie, Debbie and Jamie, and Jill Tait, who watched Tiffany on the dance floor with a sad smile. Jill took Melanie's hand. "We had no idea Melanie. No idea that Tiffany was our granddaughter. We've missed her first six years, but we plan to make them up to her, and you, from now on."

Melanie kissed Jill on the cheek. "I had such a crush on Greg when we were young. I thought I was his girlfriend, followed him to Sydney. If I had been braver. Stood up to him. Maybe ...?"

"It's not your fault Melanie. You may have been the first girl he assaulted, but we now know there were others. We did not understand he had been in trouble in Sydney. He didn't retire from football. He was 'let go' for bad behaviour. We didn't know about his relationship with you. How he controlled you, threatened harm to Tiffany." Jill shook her head. "Where did we go wrong with him? And then, to learn he was working with Rosewood Beef, forcing people already struggling in the drought to sell their land. At least some of them have returned, bought their farms back at less than they sold them. And we have had good rain."

Jill turned to Rose and Angus. "But we can never prove he

caused Charlie's heart attack, Rose, we are so sorry." Jill wiped her eyes with a handkerchief.

Rose patted her hand and murmured "It's Ok Jill. We're Ok now."

Jamie, holding his bride's hand, looked at Rose. "You stood up to him Rose. You always did, even when we were young. You are a brave woman, and we love you."

Rose turned to Melanie, smiling. "Melanie's the brave one. You saved me that night Melanie. Saved all of us."

Blushing, Melanie nodded at Rose. "Stop it. We've talked about this enough. It's a beautiful evening. Dance with your boyfriend."

Angus pulled Rose into his arms, moving her effortlessly back on to the dance floor. "Boyfriend? Really? Is that how I'm known around here? Rose Gordon's boyfriend?"

"I'm not keen on partner. How about lover? Will that work for you?" Rose giggled.

"Nup. I'm not liking any of those. How about fiancée? How does that sound? I can hear them now. There goes that Angus bloke, you know, the Vet. He's Rose Gordon's fiancée."

"Is this a proposal Angus Hamilton? About bloody time! Are you going to legitimise our child?" Rose placed her hand on her bump, looking up at Angus through her lashes.

Angus stopped for a moment, disregarding the other couples dancing around them. "I love you Rose. You are the strongest, smartest woman I know. You are beautiful. You are carrying my child and I've loved you since the day we first met. Marry me Rose."

Rose hesitated. "Do you think?.."

"Do I think what Rose? Just answer me. I'm serious."

"Do you think Charlie knew what he was doing, after all?"

EPILOGUE

Rose wiped her tears, before re-reading the letter, written laboriously in her father's hand. Dated the day of his death. She found it in the back of the last farm ledger. It looked like it had been read many times.

Dear Dad

I'm sorry to do this, but my life has no meaning without Helen. I've created a huge financial mess for myself, which I could deal with if it only affected me. But I can't bear to see the disappointment in your eyes, and Mum's, although I know you try to hide it.

To know you may lose Barrington because of me is too much to bear. It's your legacy. It's for Rose and those who come after her. I've taken that from her, from you. I'm not strong enough to go on, knowing that.

I used to think you had forced me to stay on the farm instead of following my dream of flying. Losing your two older brothers in WWII left you with a fear of flying and the only heir to Barrington. From an early age I knew it was my duty to stay and run the prop-

erty with you. Having Helen in my life, and later Rose, made i *easier. My passion for planes prevented me from making a home o* *my own for Helen and Rose, as I should have.*

Your generosity provided a beautiful home for us at Barrington but it also created a prison, of sorts. Every year that passed saw me yearning for more time in the air, which I saw as my freedom. Buying that last plane, after learning of Helen's cancer, was an expense I couldn't afford. Not insuring it was a criminal mistake. I never truly thanked you for taking a mortgage over Barrington to cover its loss, after the fire. It's a mistake Rose may pay for, long after I have gone.

Just one thing Dad. I now realise that flying was just a hobby, as it should have been. Barrington was my life, my work, my love. I've realised this too late and it is something I wish I had told you in person. If you can hang on to the farm, please give Rose time to decide what she really wants. She is studying now and I think she will go to the city for her career. If you can, leave her the option to return as I see more of you in her, than myself. Hang on if you can Dad, for Rose and her children, and theirs after that.

Jim

THE END

ACKNOWLEDGEMENTS

Without the encouragement of my girls, this book would never have been completed. Thank you Jasmine and Emily. Thank you also to Bloke, for the many weekends spent on your own while I wrote, and for listening to my excitement, and sometimes frustration, during the Charlie's Will journey.

Huge thank you to my first beta readers; Margaret Hortz (and Phil). Your comments and guidance helped create a better story than the original. Second beta readers; Helen Grant and Narah Benn provided encouragement and valuable comment. Big, big thank you to my friend and fellow author Sue Goldstiver, who offered to beta read but gave me so much more. Thank you for questioning, mentoring and celebrating with me.

The beautiful cover art was created by my dear friend Fiona Hayes @fionahayesart. Thank you for the many chats and movie dates during the creation of this book.

ABOUT THE AUTHOR

Susan Mackie grew up on a small farm in south Gippsland (Victoria) and a slightly larger irrigation property not far from the Murray River in New South Wales. She worked in Melbourne and Sydney in newspapers and printing, before moving into tourism in the upper Hunter (Barrington) region. She later moved to the Queensland Gold Coast, working in real estate before returning to publishing, tourism and later State Government. Susan has two daughters, now fully grown, and lives in a country town in south east Queensland with Bloke. Charlie's Will is the first novel in her Barrington series. The second book will be published later in 2020.

www.susanmackie.com

Ingram Content Group UK Ltd.
Milton Keynes UK
UKHW011814060423
419751UK00004B/160

9 780648 718